FURY'S MANTLE

A FURY UNBOUND NOVEL
BOOK 5

YASMINE
NEW YORK TIMES BESTSELLING AUTHOR
GALENORN

A Nightqueen Enterprises LLC Publication

Published by Yasmine Galenorn
PO Box 2037, Kirkland WA 98083-2037
FURY'S MANTLE
A Fury Unbound Novel
Copyright © 2018 by Yasmine Galenorn
First Electronic Printing: 2018 Nightqueen Enterprises LLC
First Print Edition: 2018 Nightqueen Enterprises
Cover Art & Design: Ravven
Editor: Elizabeth Flynn
Map Design: Yasmine Galenorn
Map Layout: Samwise Galenorn

A Nightqueen Enterprises LLC Publication
Published in the United States of America

Acknowledgments

I'm really glad people have been wanting more Fury—and I'm thrilled to offer you another volume in her world!

Thanks to my usual crew: Samwise, my husband, Andria and Jennifer—without their help, I'd be swamped; to the women who have helped me find my way in indie, you're all great; and to Fury herself—who started long ago as a glimmer of an idea, and who wasn't allowed out of her cage till I escaped from mine. I honestly never thought I'd be able to write these books, but thanks to technology and the courage to step out on my own, here they are.

Also, my love to my furbles, who keep me happy. And most reverent devotion to Mielikki, Tapio, Ukko, Rauni, and Brighid, my spiritual guardians and guides.

If you wish to reach me, you can find me through my website at Galenorn.com and be sure to sign up for my newsletter to keep updated on all my latest releases!

And a reminder: if you love my books, please think about leaving reviews!

Brightest Blessings,
~The Painted Panther~
~Yasmine Galenorn~

Welcome to Fury's Mantle

Wheel dashed up top to check how Thor was doing, and to bring back the storage bags. He returned, a look of alarm on his face. "There are a lot of zombies up there, but Thor's managing to hold them off."

"I've got news for you—there are more zombies on the way here, too. I just scouted ahead in the basement. There's a broken door from what used to be the building upstairs. Looks like they can smell or hear us." Zed pointed toward the far end of the basement, which was out of range of the light spell. "You might want to move it."

I nodded. "Get busy, people. Don't bother looking at the dates, just fill these bags up." I grabbed a bag and headed toward the nearest shelf. It was filled with bandages and supplies. As I swept armfuls into the bag, I wondered if the trip had really been worth it. Most medicines expired after a certain time. But then again, a number of things—like the bandages and splints and even some of the packaged foods still here—had long shelf lives. I quit worrying and just began filling my bag.

As we worked our way through the shelves, handing bags to Wheel and Elan to run up to Thor, I suddenly heard something on the other side of the shelf that I was working on. I dropped my bag and quickly drew Xan, swinging around the other side. But it wasn't a zombie I was facing. Instead, scrambling for a hole in the wall was a little girl. At least I thought it was a girl. I dove, grabbing hold of her arm and yanking her back toward me. She was clutching a pocket knife and she swiped at me. I caught her arm before she could slice me and squeezed just hard enough to make her drop the knife. She whimpered but then crumpled, as if resigned to whatever fate I had in store for her.

Map of the Seattle Area
Post—Second World Shift

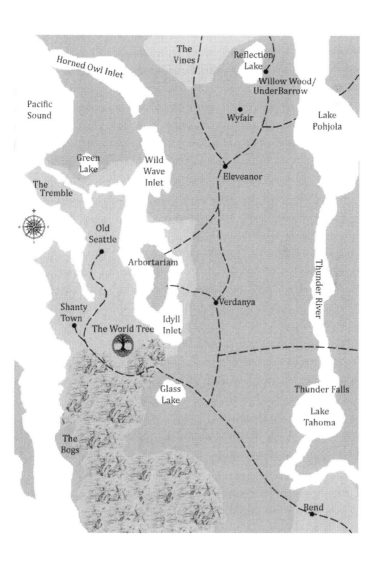

Horned Owl Inlet

The Vines

Reflection Lake

Willow Wood/ UnderBarrow

Pacific Sound

Wyfair

Lake Pohjola

Green Lake

Wild Wave Inlet

The Tremble

Eleveanor

Old Seattle

Arbortariam

Shanty Town

The World Tree

Idyll Inlet

Verdanya

Thunder River

Glass Lake

Thunder Falls

Lake Tahoma

The Bogs

Bend

The Second World Shift

THE END OF civilization as we knew it arrived not with a whimper, but with a massive storm. When Gaia—the great mother and spirit of the Earth—finally woke from her slumber to discover the human race destroying the planet through a series of magical Weather Wars, she pitched a fit. The magical storm she unleashed ripped open the doors on the World Tree. In that one cataclysmic moment, known as the World Shift, life changed forever as creatures from our wildest dreams—and nightmares—began to pour through the open portals.

The old gods returned and set up shop. The Fae and the Weres came out from the shadows and took their place among the humans. The Theosians began to appear. Technology integrated with magic, and everything became jumbled together. Nothing in the old order remained untouched.

But as time has proven over and over again, greed won out. Once again, we ignored history. This time, we started the destruction ourselves, with a storm of unimaginable devastation that swept through the world. Yes, our kind started it, but Gaia finished it.

Back to the ashes. Back to the roots. Back to the drawing board. And now, we're rebuilding anew, hoping to avoid the mistakes of the past. But dangers are rife, and in the untamed wilds, there are still madmen and would-be conquerors waiting for their chance.

Sometimes, change takes a long time to play out.

Chapter 1

My name is Queen Kaeleen the Fury. I stand at the Crossroads, bathed in the glory of Hecate's fire, overseeing a field of ash and bone.

Eight years ago, I married my love—Lord Tam, the King of UnderBarrow. In the time since the second World Shift, we have healed a great many wounds and are focused on rebuilding our world.

Willow Wood has become our new home and we've done our best to help our people grow and thrive. Life has been good the past few years. But there are dangers everywhere in this new world, and even as we strive to keep the peace, there are times when I can sense dark forces waiting just over the horizon. I may be a queen now, but I haven't been able to hang up my whip and sword. And the fire still burns within me.

I STOOD AT the top of the hill, shading my eyes as I stared over the barren fields below. I wasn't sure what I was searching for, but I had been somehow prompted to ride out here, and I wanted to know what had called to me. But there was nothing to see. The crops had been harvested and there was little going on below, except for some gleaners gathering stray bits of wheat and corn.

I turned my gaze toward the horizon.

There was a tang in the air, one that was growing more familiar with each year. We had long passed the first descent into autumn, and were approaching the storm season as the rains began to pour and the chill in the air left our breath visible.

To my right, from beyond the hills behind Reflection Lake, clouds gathered, dark and heavy with moisture. They wouldn't be here for another few hours, but when they hit, the rains promised to drench the Wild Wood and everything in it. Grateful we had brought in the last of the harvest a week ago, I shivered as a gust swept past, whipping at my legs. Rain and hail could bring famine if they hit while the crops were still in the fields, and we struggled each year to let the crops grow long enough to ripen, but not long enough to be pummeled by rain and hail.

Once again, the sense of uneasiness hit me. There was something different about this storm, though I couldn't quite put my finger on it. The hairs on the back of my neck were standing up, a sensation that reminded me of when an Abomination was near. But my Trace screen showed no sign of any Aboms, and truth was, they had been coming fewer and farther between over the past couple years. Hecate said they were still arriving via the World Tree, but the creatures wandered off in different directions, and seldom made their way up here to Willow Wood.

"Your Majesty?" Zed had been standing back, leaving me to my thoughts, but now the guard stepped forward. Dressed in the official colors of UnderBarrow—indigo, plum, and silver—he was loyal to a fault. In the years he had been attending me, I had grown to like and understand the Bonny Fae. Zed had a good mind, and more than once I thought his talents had been wasted in the Guard, but he loved his job so I kept my thoughts to myself.

"Yes?" I turned, giving one last glance to the fields below, where the gleaners hurried to finish before the weather hit. Tam and I gave them permission to pick through the fields once they were harvested. It was foolish to waste food, and some families had more children than others, so we encouraged them to forage in order to add to the allotment they received every month.

"We should get back to UnderBarrow. The light is going and the sun will set before long," he said, glancing around.

Absently, I nodded, my thoughts still on the approaching storm. Yes, there was something off about it, and if Hecate had taught me one thing, it was to pay attention to my intuition. But unable to suss out what was amiss, I finally let out a sigh and shook my head.

"Right. Let's head back, then." I turned to follow him back to the horses. Captain, my horse, was a Theosian as well. Only he was trapped in his horse form when he was on land. I had met him in his form as Captain Varga, when he had owned a ship. He was bound to Poseidon, as I was to Hecate, and when he was on a boat, he could take human form. But the moment he touched solid ground, he turned into a beautiful white stallion.

After the second World Shift, Varga had opted to live in his horse form rather than risk life on the open ocean with so many unknowns. We had become good friends, and at least once every couple of weeks we ventured out on Reflection Lake on a raft specifically made to hold a horse, where he would shift into human form and we would talk about everything and anything.

I swung my leg over his back, settling into the saddle, and Captain turned to follow Zed as we rode east along the trail to Willow Wood. The trails were navigable for the most part, and we did our best to keep them that way. But even though we had done our best to clear out the dangerous plants, it was best to stick to the paths when traveling. Wandering Ivy and Honey Sickles grew thick around here. Carnivorous plants were well-adapted to this area, and it was all too easy to wander into a patch, not realizing it until it was too late and you became so much plant food.

As we approached the village, we arrived just

in time to witness the early evening bustle. Shoppers hurried from one store to another to finish their tasks before the shops closed, and the Market Faire was shutting down for the day, the vendors packing it in to go home for supper. The lights marking the street intersections were coming on. Generally, the illumination would last until midnight, powered by the spells of UnderBarrow's techno-mages. While we couldn't produce power for the entire village, we had managed to generate enough to provide lighting on the main streets and lights for the Healers Hall.

Willow Wood had expanded from the tight little knot of survivors who had founded it and was now a thriving community of over eight hundred people, not counting the five or six hundred living in UnderBarrow itself.

The first year, we had started with a population of about two hundred who had managed to make their way out of the devastation that had been Seattle. Where the rest of the survivors went, we had no clue, but we had settled in here, on the shores of Reflection Lake. Tam moved UnderBarrow here, and we did our best to create a welcoming but orderly community. Over the years, others had found their way through the sprawling wilderness to join us.

There had been plenty of rubble with which to build new houses, and plenty of groundwater to establish the wells we needed. The first few years, we had sent raiding parties to Seattle to plunder whatever we could find in order to strengthen our position, but now we seldom went to the dead city.

There were too many zombies, too many ghosts haunting the ruins, and the dangers outweighed the prospect of what we might gain. Most of the agroline was gone, and with its demise, the cars we had once used were nothing more than rusted heaps of metal, abandoned on what was left of the roadways.

As Zed and I passed the school, the children began to file out. During the late spring and summer, they helped out in the fields like everyone else. But during late autumn and winter, they spent full days in school as the teachers crammed all the knowledge they could into them.

As soon as they saw me, the children stopped, coming to attention along with their teachers. In a wave, they knelt as I passed by.

I had gotten used to the attention, and had finally, at Tam's urging, accepted it as my right.

"You'll never be a proper queen unless you willingly take on the mantle of leadership, my love," he had said when I protested that it felt odd and uncomfortable. "You accepted marriage into the Court of UnderBarrow. Now, you must accept the responsibilities that go with it."

And I had come to terms with those duties and responsibilities, as I realized that he was correct—I had married not just my lover, but a throne and a crown.

One of the littlest girls looked up, her eyes wide, and she broke formation by waving at me. As her teacher reached for her shoulder, I lifted my hand and waved back. The teacher hesitated, then simply nodded at me with a smile.

Zed and I passed through the rest of the village and then turned south onto the path leading toward UnderBarrow proper. Another fifteen minutes saw us to the walls of UnderBarrow just as the clouds broke and rain began to pound down. I slipped off Captain and patted his muzzle, and my private stable hand took him away.

Zed opened the door for me. We were home.

"DID YOU FIGURE out what's been troubling you?" Tam asked as I stripped off my wet clothes, trading them for a pair of dry leather shorts, a V-neck long-sleeved tank, and a sweater that Patrice, my lady's maid, brought me. She gathered up my wet clothes and dropped them into the laundry basket, then held up my brush and waited silently by my vanity.

I slid on my shorts and the tank, tucking the hem into the shorts before I threaded a leather belt through the loops. Not quite the costume of a queen, but then again, we didn't live in a storybook world where the queens sat like china dolls on their thrones while the brave knights went out to slay dragons.

"No, though I could feel the uneasiness even stronger while I was out there. Whatever's on the horizon seems to be coming in with the storms, but I couldn't get a good bead on it. I'll talk to Hecate tomorrow about it. I'm supposed to meet her

7

after breakfast." I paused. "By the way, the gleaners have almost picked the fields clean. I think in a couple days we should be able to turn them under for the year."

I pulled the sweater over my head, welcoming the warmth. UnderBarrow was always on the cool side, especially as summer moved into autumn when the temperature of the days still fluctuated. But it was nearly time to start lighting the hearthfire in our quarters.

Tam came up behind me, circling my waist with his arms as he leaned down to nuzzle my neck. He was King of UnderBarrow, and king of my heart, as well. Tall and lithe, he moved in a sinuous dance, his gestures as graceful and smooth as his voice. His hair fell in a tangle of curls to his waist, and he held it smoothed back from his face with a silver barrette. His eyes were silver, ringed with black, and he was muscled but taut and firm. His lips bowed in a way that made me want to kiss him every time I looked at him. We had been together almost nine years, and each day, I thanked the gods he was in my life.

He kissed my ear, then whispered, "I want you."

"I want you, too," I said. "But I want to take my time with you, and we're supposed to meet the others in less than twenty minutes."

I glanced at the clock. It was set to run on outworld time, not UnderBarrow time. It helped me keep track of my days better. The Bonny Fae had a natural affinity for knowing how much time had passed—both outside their realm and within it. But I was Theosian—a minor goddess—and I didn't have that internal sensor.

"All right. But later, you're mine and all mine," Tam said, spinning me in his arms. He pressed his lips to mine, and all thoughts of time and Abominations and dinner went out the window as I melted into his kiss. His lips were warm, sensuous against mine, and it felt like he was trying to drink me up, dive deep into my soul and become one with me.

As he let go, I came up for air, gasping. "Damn, you don't give a girl a chance, do you?"

He smiled, the corners of his lips tilting up. "When it comes to you, no. I don't ever want you to regret marrying me, Fury."

I sat down at the vanity. Patrice was smiling, but she said nothing. The ideal lady's maid, she knew how to keep from intruding on private moments, all the time being there whenever I needed her. Now, she began to brush out my hair, toweling it dry and then braiding it back.

I watched in the mirror as she smoothed the wayward curls. My hair was black, with crimson flames running through it. My eyes were dark brown—coffee straight up, please. I touched up my makeup when she finished braiding my hair, then she carefully placed my circlet around my head, affixing it snuggly. I wore it when I wasn't in the throne room, saving my "fancy" crown for official gatherings and functions.

I sat back, eyeing myself. "Thanks, Patrice."

"What shoes do you want, milady?"

"I think the Umbiargo ankle boots. They're comfortable and warm." I waited till she brought them, then held out my feet for her to put them on me. I had learned to accept her help, because it was her job and she was glad to have it, so I quit fidgeting a long time back.

Tam was ready to go by the time Patrice finished. He had a valet, but usually dismissed him and fared for himself.

I stood. "Thank you. Go get yourself some dinner. We'll probably be a couple hours at least. I'll ring for you when I return."

She curtseyed, then hurried to the door to open it for us. "As you will, milady."

As Tam and I exited our chambers, Zed and Sig—another one of our personal guards—were there, waiting to escort us to our private dining hall.

WHEN WE ENTERED the room, we found Elan and Jason already there. We gathered around the intimate dining table, taking our seats.

"Are Hans and Greta making it tonight?" I asked.

Elan nodded. "Yes, though I think they'll be a little late. Hans had his sword-mastery class tonight at New Valhalla, and on the nights he teaches, he always runs a little late." Elan was one of my personal guards, but she was also one of my best friends, and the wife of yet another best friend.

Jason yawned and stretched. He looked tired.

"What a day. I cannot believe how busy the store is. When we were in Seattle, I made okay money, but here, business is booming with a fraction of the population. Dream Wardens is doing a good business." He paused. "I've had a lot of folks coming in offering to barter, though. How long before you think the new currency will catch on?"

Tam shrugged. "I don't know. But people have to accept it sooner or later. We have to have an equitable system of commerce if we're going to grow. I'll address it at the next community meeting." While we seldom scheduled mandatory meetings for the town, we did require at least one member of the household in attendance for our monthly meetings. That brought it down to a manageable size. And households could be considered roommates living together, or family groupings.

"How's Aila doing?" Usually Elan and Jason brought their daughter with them, but tonight she was conspicuously absent.

"She's studying for a big test tomorrow." Elan grinned. "She's determined to pass with honors this year. I promised if she maintains a B average, she can return to taking lessons with Rika."

Rika was the head of training for the UnderBarrow Guard, and she taught martial arts classes for children on the side. Aila showed a remarkable aptitude for just about anything requiring bodywork, but she also had a tendency to let her schoolwork slide. Elan yanked her out of Rika's training class as a last resort to get her to pay attention to her studies.

Jason snorted. "If anything lights a fire under

her, this will. She moped all summer because she knew we weren't going to let her go back to training until she brings home a full B average for an entire semester." He smiled more often now, something I was grateful to see. It had been eight years since he had been trapped in the realm of Chaos, and he had finally cracked through most of the shellshock and learned to enjoy life again.

We chatted about this and that, and within twenty minutes, Greta and Hans hustled in. Both looked like they could use a good shower. Even Greta's wings looked droopy. They joined us, apologizing for being late, and dinner got under way.

We were halfway through the meal when Zed approached the table, looking apologetic. "Your Majesties, we have a problem."

Tam glanced up at him, frowning. "What's wrong?"

"There's been an attack off the road leading north, just outside the gates that mark UnderBarrow's territory."

I set down my bread. "What kind of attack?"

Zed glanced at Elan, Jason, Hans, and Greta. He knew they were safe to talk around, unless we told him otherwise, so he took a deep breath and spread a map on the table as we made space. He pointed to the northern gates, then traced a line a little off to the left, by the side of the lake.

"Here. Two of our villagers were returning from hunting when they came across the scene. It took them an hour to make it back to Willow Wood through the rain. Why they didn't tell the guards at the gate, I don't know, but apparently they decided that they should tell us directly."

"Yes, yes, go on." I sighed. We were still trying to get the villagers to accept the town guard
as authority figures. They were falling in line, but
most everybody had been used to living in a big
city, where talking to the authorities could get you
locked up, or worse.

"They found the remains of a group of campers
at a campsite. There's a makeshift cart, though it
looks like they were pulling it by hand. And the
remains of whoever was making camp, as well."

"How many dead?" Tam asked.

"That's the thing. They don't know." He paused,
the expression on his face shifting. "Your Majesty,
when I say 'remains'...I mean *remains*. It looks like
an entire camping party was ravaged. There were
bits and pieces of bodies everywhere. There's no
telling how many victims there were. The hunters were afraid to stay in case whatever destroyed
the camp should return. They hurried as fast as
they could back to Willow Wood and then here, to
UnderBarrow."

I dabbed my lips with my napkin and then
pushed back my plate. Spaghetti didn't seem like
such a good idea after all. "Did they recognize...
anyone?"

Zed shook his head. "No, there wasn't enough
light left to discern anything more than the attack
had been wholesale carnage. But the scent of blood
was heavy in the air. We've dispatched a group
of guards to check it out. They're fully armed, of
course. It sounds a nasty piece of business."

I sat back, toying with my napkin. The energy

leapt and crackled around me, and I could feel the same unease that I had felt during the afternoon as I watched over the fields. I wanted to go out there with the guards, to look around to see if I could sense anything. I thought of asking Tam, but I knew what he'd say. There had been times over the past few years when I had disobeyed his wishes. Hecate's orders came first, and he accepted that. But he wouldn't want me going out without her blessing, given the danger involved.

As I looked up, he was staring at me. "You want to go along."

I blushed. "It's not that I *want* to, but..." I turned to the others. "You might as well know. I woke up with the feeling that something is dread-fully wrong. It bothered me most of the morning until I finally took Zed and we went out to the lake, overlooking the wheat fields."

"Did you figure out what it was?" Elan asked. She, like the others, took my premonitions seri-ously. "Was it an Abom?"

I shook my head. "No, actually, it wasn't. I don't know what caused the sensation, but once we were there, the certainty that something *is* wrong grew. I couldn't shake it off. The moment Zed began talking about the attack, that feeling returned full force. I think that whatever I was sensing earlier is connected to this attack."

Tam pressed his lips together for a moment. Then, he shrugged. "You're probably right. You usually are. But it's late, and there's a storm at hand. The campground is an hour's ride there and back, at the very least. I think, given there's someone skulking around who has the ability to destroy a campground filled with people, it's not in our best interests to check it out in the dark."

"You're letting the guards go," I said, but immediately knew that was a mistake.

"They're trained for it."

"So am I."

"Be that as it may, *you're* not expendable. Let's wait till we know what we're dealing with before we take action. We would just be in the way and the guards would be torn between looking for whoever did this and protecting us." Tam reached out to take my hand. He gazed at me long and hard, and the weight of his years of experience and life washed through me.

I let out a sigh. "Very well. I'll wait. But tomorrow, we go look. And tonight, we stay up until the guards have a report for us. Deal?"

"Deal." Tam turned to Zed. "Update us with whatever you find out, no matter how important or unimportant the information seems to be. And keep an eye on the remains. Zombies have made their way over to the Wild Wood from old Seattle. You never can tell what's going to happen when you're dealing with the undead."

With that, he dismissed Zed and turned back to dinner.

Tam gestured. "Please, finish your meal."

We all returned to our food but my heart wasn't in it. Instead, alarms were ringing loud and clear that—whatever this was—we weren't done with it yet, and we weren't even remotely prepared for what was behind it.

BY MIDNIGHT, ELAN and Jason had gone home, but Greta and Hans hung around to find out what the guards had to report. We were curled up in our private chambers, talking while we waited for the men to check in. I was leaning against Tam's chest, while Hans was rubbing Greta's feet. I treasured these moments when we could just be ourselves with our closest friends, without having to put on a face for the public.

"Freya has set me in charge of harvesting. It's daunting," Greta said. She was a Valkyrie, still a relatively new one, and lately she had been working nonstop for her goddess. Freya was a tough boss. I was grateful I was bound to Hecate and not the Norse bombshell.

"What's the difference between harvesting souls and escorting them to Valhalla?" I was still fuzzy on the whole "gather the souls" bit. I dispatched Aboms and sent them back to Pandoriam, their plane. I had little to do with spirits except for Queet, my spirit guide, who was currently taking a much-needed vacation. Queet had been testy lately to the point where I begged Hecate to give him some time off.

"Escorting souls to Valhalla means welcoming them to their afterlife and guiding them so they don't lose their way. Harvesting souls comes on the behest of Odin and is a lot trickier." She cupped her goblet of mead and shivered. "When Odin orders us to harvest a soul, we have to take them. Meaning...they aren't dead yet."

"Meaning you have to kill them?" I asked, lowering my voice.

She nodded, staring starkly at the fire. "There's always a good reason, but it's not like fighting a battle against someone trying to kill you. Or like taking out a monster. These are people who, for whatever reason, need to die. The Norns tell Odin, and he tells us. It's part of the job I never really thought about much before I went through the ritual. We aren't taught about it in our training. We only come to learn it after our flying-up ceremonies."

I glanced over at Hans. He took her hand. It was difficult for him to put his arm around her shoulders, given she had massively beautiful raven's wings, but he held tight to her fingers, bringing them to his lips for a kiss.

"Tell them, honey," he said.

Greta closed her eyes for a moment, then hiccupped and took a deep breath. "Today I had to take the soul of a mother of five. She has five children under the age of ten, and they were there. I had to take her soul and watch as her body fell right in the midst of those children. The Norns insist it's necessary—her thread came to an end, and for whatever reason, it was time to cut her free. But that didn't make it any easier. Even though they didn't see me, I could see the faces of her kids, and it just tore my heart up. Sometimes I wonder if I'm tough enough for this job."

"What does Freya say about it?" These were tricky waters. There were times I'd had to do things I didn't feel good about, but Hecate had bade me to do them. And there were memories that I did my best to leave in the past, where they belonged.

"Just that I'll develop the ability to be unbiased in the future. *Detached*, she called it. But I'm not certain I want to be detached to something like that. I guess what I want doesn't matter, though. There's no going back. There's no walking out." She rubbed her head, then let out another sigh. "Thanks for listening. It helps to talk about it where I know I'm not going to be attacked for either being too weak, or being a murderer."

And *that* was something I understood even more. Anyone not bound to the gods had no clue of what it meant when they required you to do something that went against your nature. It didn't happen often, but when it did, it made for all sorts of inner conflict.

I was about to offer her another drink when someone knocked on the door. We were drinking mead made by the UnderBarrow brewers. It was stronger than most hard liquors I had tasted. I put down the bottle as Dara—our housekeeper—answered.

She led Zed into the living room and I instantly set the bottle back down.

"You have news?" I asked.

He looked shaken. "Yes, Your Majesty."

Tam slowly straightened, brushing his hair back from his face. "What did you find out?"

Zed looked so pale that I motioned to the otto-man near the sofa. "Sit. Dara, please get a glass for him. I think he needs a drink."

Zed shook his head. "No, thank you, Your Majes-ty, although I could use a cup of tea and something to eat."

"Tea and a sandwich, please." I motioned to the housekeeper and she vanished without a word. "Zed, what's wrong?"

"My men figured out just how many were at the camp. We know that there were at least six adults and five children in the camp. That's as much as we could put together from what...remained. There may be more in the undergrowth and forest around the campsite. The guards will look again in the morning."

Zed looked queasy and I didn't blame him. It was bad enough dealing with the remains of adults, but children? Far more difficult.

"Could it have been a pack of zombies?" Hans asked.

Zed shrugged. "We're not certain. There's very little we actually know except that right now, something big enough to destroy an entire camp-ing party is out there, and it looks like whatever it is was hungry. The remains were gnawed on," he added.

Tam sat very still for a moment, then glanced at me. "Come. We should sleep. We'll get dressed and go out there at first light with the guards."

I nodded, thinking that whatever it was I had been feeling, it had struck. And it wasn't done. That much I knew to the very core of my gut.

Chapter 2

MORNING CAME TOO early. I blinked when Patrice woke me. As I slowly pushed myself up against the headboard, huddling under the covers, I realized that Tam wasn't there.

"Where's Lord Tam?" I asked, yawning.

"He's been up for an hour. He's in the Blue room, talking to the guards, milady. He asks that you join him as soon as you're dressed. He said you'll find breakfast there." But she was holding out a cup of tea.

I took it, practically inhaling it, grimacing as I nearly burned my tongue. Cupping my hands around my mug, I slid into the slippers Patrice had laid out for me and padded over to my dressing table. She had laid out my leather shorts, a sturdy long-sleeved sweater, and my leather jacket.

"You win the award for prognosticating fashion needs," I said with a laugh, placing my cup on the vanity. "I don't have time for a bath, but that's all right. I'll take an extra-long one tonight."

She began to brush my hair, parting it to plait it back. I stared at myself in the mirror. It had been a long road to get to where I was, one fraught with pain and loss and danger.

I was thirty-eight years old, young by Theosian standards. But it felt like I had already lived two lifetimes over, and had started in on another. The first had been when I was a child. That was cut short when my mother and I were kidnapped by a serial killer and I was forced to watch him kill her. The second had been from the time I was fifteen until I was thirty. Jason had taken care of me after my mother's death, and I had lived in Darktown, in Seattle, guided by Hecate, focused on killing Abominations that crossed over through the World Tree. I had never given much thought to the future, but then the future hit me in the face when I had fallen in love with Tam. And everything had shifted again as the third stage of my life had begun. We had fled the destruction of the second World Shift, heading into the Wild Wood and making our way here, where we established Willow Wood. I had married Tam and become Queen of UnderBarrow. And we had settled in to make a new life for ourselves.

Everything had been peaceful—more or less. I had learned the ways of the Bonny Fae and did my best to adapt to them. And Tam's people had adapted to me. Willow Wood thrived under our rule, and we began to put our former lives behind us as we carved out a niche in the new world. It hadn't been easy, especially giving up the comforts of civilization, but we had managed and adapted, and learned to stay focused on necessities. Survival was not a macroscopic concept—not on a small-scale level—and definitely not on a day-to-day basis. But with this new threat, perhaps it was time to start looking at the bigger picture. Perhaps it was time to branch out again, to send scouts out, to look beyond the borders of our territory.

"What are you thinking about, milady? You look so solemn." Patrice finished with my hair and then held out my clothes to me. We had worked out a system that kept me from feeling like a china doll, yet kept her from feeling expendable. She would lace my corsets when I wore them and she laced up my boots, and did my hair. But I put on my daily clothes by myself, allowing her to hand them to me as I was ready for them. Ornamental robes, I welcomed her help with.

As she laced up my boots, I said, "Long thoughts, Patrice. I'm just thinking about the past, and how it's brought us to the present. And about where we're headed for the future. We've had skirmishes before, but the look on Zed's face last night, and the uneasiness I'm feeling in my bones, makes me think it's time to step outside our borders and take a look around."

I dipped my head, allowing her to fix my circlet on my head before I fingered the golden "F" pendant that hung from its chain around my neck. I never took off the necklace. Hecate had given it to me herself, and it was a tangible connection between us.

"I need to visit Hecate today. To ask her if she has any insight to what's going on. I'll do so when we get back. Can you ask a page to run a message up to Gudarheim to ask if she's ready to meet?"

Patrice nodded. "Of course, milady. What else do you need?" she asked as she helped me on with my leather jacket. I had plundered enough jackets from Seattle that, unless I either gained or lost a lot of weight, I'd have enough to last me through several hundred years, providing they were stored correctly.

I sighed. "I need my sword and dagger. I'm not about to go out there unarmed."

Truth be told, I was never unarmed. I glanced down at my right leg. I was wearing leather shorts. My usual garb, they allowed me access to the tattoo of a flaming whip that ran down the right side of my leg, from thigh to ankle. Hecate had inked it herself on me, and when I slapped my hand against the handle of the whip, it came off my leg, ready to use. It had been awhile since I'd been called on to wield it, but I still practiced with it three times a week, as well as working out five days a week to keep in shape.

As Patrice fit my scabbard over my back, adjusting it so I could detach it for easy access, I sucked in a long breath as I focused myself into battle mode. It had been awhile since I'd had to wield Xan—my sword—outside of practice. I could feel her waking up, almost hungry for a good shake-down.

Patrice handed me my dagger sheath, and I strapped it around my left thigh and slid my blade into it. I slipped on fingerless gloves. They were lightweight and flexible, and I had discovered how much easier it was to handle my weapons with them.

"Ready?" Patrice asked, standing back, looking at me.

I nodded. "Yeah, I'm ready." And I realized, I was. I missed the hunt...the chase.

She opened the door for me. "I'll be here if you need me."

I turned to her as I slipped out the door to where Elan was waiting for me.

"I know, and I'm grateful." With a smile, I followed Elan into UnderBarrow, to the Blue room, to talk strategy.

TAM WAS THERE, waiting, along with Damh Varias—Tam's second in command. Hans was there, as well as Zed, and a couple of other guards. Elan and I took our places as one of the serving maids brought me a plate of eggs, bacon, apple-sauce, a large roll, and cheese. She returned with a cup of tea for me, and then retreated to the corner of the room to await orders.

As soon as Elan and I had settled into our seats, Tam cleared his throat, which was all it took to silence the room. "Zed, did the guards find anything else during the night?"

Zed shrugged. "A few more remains that makes

it look like we may have had more casualties than we first thought. Also, one of the guards recognized...one of the heads we found."

"Heads?" Elan asked, a grim look on her face.

"Yes, it appears that the entire group of victims was savaged. There are bite marks and enough flesh missing that we can reasonably assume that the attackers ate them. The heads were untouched, but their internal organs appear to be missing, as well as big chunks of flesh." Zed's words dropped like lead in the room.

"Who was the victim, then?"

"One of our herbalists. The guard was dating her, which made it that much worse. Ericeidae was leading a foraging expedition into the woods for a week, hunting for herbs. There are a few plants that only blossom this time of year. Windsake and throbrob are two of the ones that the healers need most during the winter to fight influenza and lungrot, and they are difficult to find. Ericeidae was one of the best foragers we had. She's going to be missed. But this does allow us to identify the missing, given we have the roster of those who were in the party. There were two more adults that we haven't found heads for." Zed looked queasy.

"Why were the children along?" Tam asked, his voice tight.

"They were on a field trip. We've checked with the school. Five of the students showed a remarkable talent with healing, and so they were allowed to go along. The classroom can't give you the direct experience that a field expedition can."

Tam nodded, his lips set in a thin line. "Word's

going to get out and there's going to be panic. Instruct Lieutenant Aerie and someone else he deems suitable to notify the families. He's good at delivering bad news. He's empathetic and has the right sensitivity."

"Yes, Your Majesty." Zed scribbled down a note.

I hung my head, not wanting to think about the children who had been along on that trip. "Could it be zombies? Seattle is filled with them. The plague wasn't wiped out like we hoped it would be, and in the intervening years, the city has developed a massive colony of them, along with ghosts and spirits and other creepers."

"Don't forget about the possibility of vampires," Tam said. "Kython and his crew have increased their numbers."

I shuddered. We had met Kython when we were headed out on the Tremble to save Tam. I had discovered that the *oh-so-famous* vampire had been a Theosian, which meant my kind could be turned. And I also learned that everything I had been taught about vampires had been a myth.

The Conglomerate—the old government—had led us to believe they engineered the vamps, but what they had actually done was capture real vampires and attempt to create a mutant variety under their control. What they had *actually* ended up doing was creating yet another monster.

Ghouls were deadly, all right, but hadn't proved submissive to their creators. Born with a blood lust and desire for flesh, ghouls could breed because they were still alive, but they usually kept to the subterranean areas of the cities—the sewers and basements.

Actual vampires were true to their legend. The living undead wasted no love for the government who had used them. It occurred to me that I still owed Kython a favor. I pushed that thought out of my mind, and focused on our immediate concerns.

"I doubt if it was vampires," I said. "They drink blood, but they don't tend toward carnage like this. Ghouls, maybe?"

"I suppose a pack of them could have made their way over from the city, around the north side between Horned Owl Inlet and Wild Wave Inlet." Tam frowned. "But that's a long way for them to travel, and while sunlight won't kill them like it does vampires, it does hurt them."

"The remains that we found are in the Healer's Hall. Do you want to see them, or should we head out to the site?" Zed asked.

My stomach lurched at the thought of looking over the remains of anybody, let alone children. I had seen my share of death over the years, and one thing I had learned: while you might get used to it, as long as you retained a shred of your humanity, you never became immune to the sight. I was grateful when Tam shook his head.

"No, there's no need to see them. At least not right at this moment. Send a page to the Healer's Hall and tell them to do their best to preserve the remains till we return. I'm certain the medics are going to have their work cut out for them anyway, piecing together what...belongs to whom." He stood. "We leave in a quarter hour. Meet back here. Take care of any personal needs, and—"

he turned to the serving girl. "Will you make up lunches for Her Majesty, myself, Dame Elan, and Lord Hans?" He glanced over at Elan. "I take Jason isn't coming?"

"He will if you ask. But you know how skittish he still can be."

Tam nodded. "Then leave him be. If we need him, he will come, but right now, we're merely on a recon mission."

As we scurried to get ready, I felt a lump in my throat. It had been several months since I had gone out hunting an Abom, and other than that, life had been focused on what felt like extremely normal activity. I had a feeling that was about to change.

CAPTAIN WAS WAITING for me, pawing the ground nervously. I patted his side and whispered softly to him. "It's all right, Cap'n. We'll be fine."

He stopped fidgeting but as I swung my leg over his back, I got the feeling he really wasn't happy with what we were doing. It crossed my mind to ask him if he sensed anything, but that would require a trip to the lake and going out on the boat, and we didn't have the time. But when I got back, I was determined to tap him for anything that he had sensed.

Tam's horse was a majestic black stallion, a Friesian. The horse's mane was as wavy as Tam's hair, and so was his tail. Aethar, the massive horse, was as noble as they came, and he looked as wild and free as Tam did. Tam rode him bareback—no saddle needed, and the horse responded to him as though they were cut from the same cloth. His feathers had been trimmed so that he wouldn't get them caught in bushes or burrs, and he gleamed under the pale dawn.

We headed out, with Zed in front, followed by two more guards. Tam and Hans rode behind them, then me—riding side by side with Elan. Four more guards brought up the rear.

We had the elite crew with us. Every guard was from the King's Force division. These were the warriors who guarded over Tam and me, and they were among the most highly skilled in the entire army. They were all Bonny Fae, except for Teragamma, a magus who was a Theosian like me, bound to the Morrígan. Five ravens flew over Teragamma's head, following the sorceress as we headed out from UnderBarrow, through Willow Wood and along the road that led north.

We had claimed a large territory, large enough to grow into without being too large to keep an eye over, and there were no other villages close enough to argue the point.

The road was mist-shrouded and foggy, and clouds rolled low along the sky, dark and billowing. The tall firs and cedars that forested the area hung heavy with rain from the night before, their scent cleansing the air as it braced me.

During the first World Shift, the forests had come back with a vengeance, and people either lived within the cities and towns or built the odd house here and there through the wooded glens. But in the eight years since the devastating tsunami and quakes that had riddled the land, as far as we knew, most of the bigger cities had fallen. Villages had sprung up, as survivors banded together to figure out a new way of life.

I thought of Tigra, a weretiger whom I had known. Five and a half years ago, she and a group of scouts had set out to cross the country, to find out how much still stood as they journeyed to the capital of Atlantea. But we hadn't heard from them since. No messages, no sign of them. I hoped that they were still alive—I liked Tigra. But I didn't hold out much faith that I'd ever see her again.

The ravens flying with Teragamma were loud, cawing as they flew, their calls echoing through the forest. The *drip, drip, drip* of rain off the trees kept up a constant spatter as we rode along in silence. Elan glanced to the side, watching the trees as we passed by.

"They aren't happy," she said after a time.

"What aren't?"

"The trees. They're feeling furtive and watchful. I've never quite sensed them so...cautious, that would be the word." She frowned, clucking at her horse. He moved toward the side of the road and Elan stopped him as she stared into the dense thicket of undergrowth. We halted, waiting for her. She cocked her head, as if listening and then, after a brief silence, turned back to us.

"There are creatures that have come through the woods, dark and angry. The trees are whispering amongst one another. I can sense their communication, but not what they are saying. But they're definitely uneasy. I think it would behoove us to pay attention and follow suit. Be cautious. Keep alert."

Zed wove through the other horses until he made his way to her side. He stared into the patch she had been watching. "Should we go off road to find out what's in there?"

She considered his question for a moment, then shook her head. "No, we'd be at a disadvantage if we came up against something. Keep to the road, but don't drift. Don't let yourselves get distracted. There is danger in these woods. I can feel it on the tip of my tongue—a sour, bitter taste."

We went back to our positions, and I clucked to my horse, speeding up the pace a little. Our horses had been trained for battle, but even they seemed restless. I was picking up on Captain's nervousness, but he held true to the path.

By the time we neared the campground where the foragers had been found massacred, we were all on edge. I could tell from Tam's stiff shoulders, and his darting gaze told me that he was taking the warnings to heart. I wanted to ride next to him, but it would only make him more concerned for my safety and throw him off his guard.

As we entered the campground, a hush fell over the area. The ravens landed in a nearby tree, but they were silent, and I noticed that there was no birdsong filling the air. A knot formed in my stomach and I drew a long breath. The scent of blood still hung heavy in the air, and the ground was stained with it everywhere I looked.

There were four guards already there examining the area, and four others keeping watch. They straightened as we approached. When they saw Tam and me, they dropped to one knee.

We dismounted, and Tam held out his hand to me. I placed my hand atop his, and we silently walked over to the senior guard, who lowered his head, then rose as Tam gestured for him to stand.

"What have you found?" Tam asked.

The guard—I recognized him as Kroix, a hawk-shifter like Jason, though I wasn't sure if he was a member of the Cast—let out a long sigh.

"Not much. But what we have discovered sets me uneasy, Your Majesty. If you would come look." He turned toward the bushes and Tam, accompanied by Zed and Hans, followed him behind a huckleberry bush.

A moment later, Tam called for me and, with Elan escorting me, I joined them. We were in the middle of a patch of waist-high ferns, but beside one of the biggest ferns, there were a couple of footprints. Well, toe prints, along with prints of the balls of someone's feet. But they weren't human, that much was obvious.

"Do you recognize what kind of prints these are?" Tam asked.

I squatted, looking at them closely. "It's difficult. They're distorted by the muddy ground. But they're larger than normal and seem...off. As though they're walking on the balls of their feet."

"We also found prints about six feet away, but they aren't of toes." Kroix motioned to another set of prints in the mud. He was right, they weren't toe prints. Instead, they looked more like indentations made by a club of some sort, though whatever it was wasn't smooth on the ends, but ridged. There were two of them and I realized they were just about as far apart as the toe prints were.

"Hands. Fists, rather. If you ball up your fists and press them into the mud..." I made a fist, holding it up for them to see.

Kroix nodded, balling his fist and leaning over to press it into the wet ground. Sure enough, when he pulled it away, the print matched the others, only it was much smaller. Something about it struck a bell and I gazed at the two sets of prints again, trying to figure out what was jogging my memory.

But Elan figured it out first. "Lycanthropes! They run on their hands and feet like that, on the balls of their feet, and on their knuckles. This spread would fit the size of an average one."

A chill raced up my spine and I remembered the fight we had been through on our way to Reflection Lake, in our haste to get away from Seattle as it drowned. She was right. That's what I had been thinking of. We had been attacked by a band of lycanthropes and they had been running on their hands and feet.

Lycanthropes were similar to Theosians in that their werewolf mothers had wandered through rogue magical spots during pregnancy, changing the DNA. Unlike Theosians, who ended up with magical gifts and pledged to the gods, lycanthropes were more wolf than they were human, and they were stuck in between, unable to transform. They were a cross between both races, human and wolf, and they could walk on their knuckles and toes. They were a terrifying race, bloody and violent, and they could breed true, which made them that much more dangerous. They also tended to feast on whatever they killed, regardless of who or what the prey had been.

"Crap. If we have a band of lycanthropes running around, we're in trouble. We better send out a hunting party to track them down so we know what we're facing." I turned to Tam. "I know there are nests of them in the woods. Maybe we should contact the Fir Mountain Pack and ask them if they've seen any lately."

Werewolves tended to dislike lycanthropes as much as they disliked vampires. The creatures reminded them of their darker sides, and when a lycanthrope was born into a Pack, they were set out to die. Usually nature took its course, but now and then one would survive.

"Good idea, though I don't like owing any favors to them, even for something so simple as information," Tam said. I could see the wheels turning in his head. "Zed, do you concur this could be a lycanthrope attack?"

Zed nodded. "Now that Elan and Her Majesty Kaeleen suggest it, I can see no other possibility. There may be another answer, but this is as good as I can think of for now."

Tam motioned for us to head back to the horses. "Then we ride for home. When we get there, I want to talk to the unit leaders from the guard, including Lt. Aerie. We need to fortify our defenses and step up watch on our borders."

As we mounted our horses, I glanced around the area. The campground had a desolate air to it and I wondered if the spirits of the dead were going to end up stuck here. I thought we'd do well to hold a village-wide ceremony for them, and have the priests from the various temples lay them to rest. But we'd have to also figure out damage control to prevent panic. Because like it or not, we couldn't just build a wall around the village and hope to survive, hiding away from the dangers that were out there.

WE'D BARELY RETURNED to Willow Wood when Hecate sent a page to find me.

"Your Majesty, her Gracious Divinity, the Lady Hecate bade me to petition you to join her as soon as you are able."

The poor boy looked about ready to wet himself. Between talking to a goddess and then to his queen, he was probably scared shitless that he'd do something wrong. Pages usually managed to handle their fear as they grew into the positions, but I knew that this child had only been at it for a few months. I remembered his mother's petition for her son to get the job.

"Very good. What's your name?"

"Elbert." Then, suddenly aware he'd flubbed, he blurted out, "Your Majesty. My name is Elbert, Your Majesty."

I wanted to smile, but Tam had taught me a great deal about truly being queen to his realm. Instead, I nodded and gravely said, "Good. You remembered. Now, don't forget again, all right?"

He worried his lip for a moment, then bowed. "Yes, Your Majesty. Thank you. Should I take a message in return?"

I shook my head. "No, I'll go now. You get on with your other errands."

As the boy sped off away from UnderBarrow, I suddenly found myself longing for the old days, when nobody knew who I was save for a select few. But even as the thought crossed my mind, I shook it away. Life had never been carefree for me, or easy. And the further I distanced myself from some of my memories, the better.

THE TEMPLE OF New Olympus had been built from marble blocks carted over from Seattle. It wasn't anywhere near as grand as Naós ton Theón had been in the Peninsula of the Gods, but it was still breathtaking. Only one story now, the temple spread out to a fair size, but the gods had down-sized their expectations.

I dashed up the steps to the massive door that had been formed of oak and walnut, and the guards standing watch opened it as I approached. I gave them a quick nod as they bent their knee, and then hurried inside.

Hecate's office was near the front of the building. Coralie was sitting in a small cubicle outside of Hecate's office. She had been Hecate's assistant for longer than I could remember, and when the temple of Naós ton Theón had still stood, her desk had been massive and exquisite. Now, she had a manual typewriter, a small marble desk, and no air conditioning. But she looked happy.

"Is she in?" I asked.

Coralie quickly stood and curtseyed. She might work for a goddess, but she knew to give the Queen of UnderBarrow her fair due. The gods extended respect—generally—when they received it. I wasn't sure if Coralie was a Theosian, or if she was divine in some other way, but I had the feeling she was anything but human.

"Yes, she's waiting for you. She said to send you straight in when you got here. Go ahead."

I tapped at the door.

"Enter."

Hecate was sitting on the corner of her desk as I entered the office.

She had furnished it with beautiful old oak furniture from a raid on Seattle, and she had her requisite leather chair, curio cabinets filled with blades and weapons, and several filing cabinets. She had her own lights, magical in nature, but then again, she was a goddess of magic as well as the goddess of the Crossroads.

Hecate was wearing a pair of black leather pants, a pale gray shirt, and a black suede jacket. She was tall—close to six feet—and her raven hair was caught back in a sleek ponytail that brushed her waist. She wore a silver diadem in front of the knot of the ponytail. The circlet reminded me of a Celtic knot, with three snakes entwining as they held aloft a crescent moon. The horns were pointed up, and in their center, a black moonstone. She fastened her gaze on me, her eyes the color of early dawn—periwinkle with hoarfrost drifting in them.

I knelt before her. Every time I laid eyes on her, my love for my lady returned in a flood of gratitude. This was the one place I truly belonged, truly felt at home—in Hecate's presence. She might ride me hard at times, but she was forever in my corner, always standing behind me, always pushing me forward.

Hecate wasted no time on small talk. "I heard about the massacre. Tell me what you know."

I frowned. For simple murders, the gods usually didn't usually get involved or pay much attention. The concerned look on her face worried me.

"Lycanthropes. It had to have been a pack of them. We're not clear on how many people were actually there—it was a group of herbalists out foraging. At least six adults and five children, as far as we know. It was bad, Hecate. Really bad." I sank onto the leather sofa in the corner, still feeling queasy. "They ate them—parts of them. The guards found body parts all over. We have to tell the village, but we have to be cautious. There's no way we want to incite widespread panic."

Hecate nodded. "How do you know it was lycanthropes?"

"Prints." I told her what we had found. "Yesterday, I sensed something was off. I was out near the wheat fields, and I sensed something on the horizon, coming in with the storms. I have no clue what, but it set me on edge. I felt the same energy where the attack happened." I paused, then added, "This reminded me of the Aboms, but yet, it didn't. I don't know how else to explain it—but it was something in the distance. A threatening force."

For a moment, she said nothing. Then Hecate straightened her shoulders and turned to her wall of blades. "There *is* something on the horizon. I don't know what yet, and neither do the others, but we can all feel it."

"Do you think Gaia might be planning another siege?"

Hecate shook her head. "No, I don't think so, though I can't be certain. Since the second World Shift, the world has grown more feral and dangerous. Gaia's weary after raining down her chaos and she slumbers, resting. The Greenlings patrol the woodlands, but only for those who would strike against the natural order."

"Then what could it be? Has something new come through the World Tree?"

The goddess walked over to the window that looked out on the woodland around the Temple of New Olympus. "Possibly." She turned, leaning her back against the glass. "Make no mistake, Fury. We're on our own. You might have thought the tsunami and quakes eight years ago were the turning point, but my visions tell me a deadly force is on the move and we're about to plunge deep into the darkness. Winter is on the way, and I just hope we can ride it out to see the spring."

Chapter 3

EVERYWHERE I TURNED, the World Shifted and quaked under my feet. I tried to stand, but the land had melted under my feet into a shifting whirlpool of color and texture. Dizzy, I felt myself being sucked into the center. I struggled to steady myself, but the moment I was stable and standing, the land shifted again. Gaia was turning in her sleep, I thought, shifting under her covers, and every time she moved, the land moved with her.

I righted myself again, trying to figure out where I was. Nothing looked familiar, and yet everywhere I looked, the sense of déjà vu followed me. I set my gaze on a pile of rocks in the middle of the stark, neon landscape, and just as soon as they began to come into focus, their shapes began to run, melting into drops that danced and skittered across the landscape.

Where the hell was I?

Queet? Queet? Are you there? But there was no answer.

I began to walk, to try to get away from the whirlpool behind me, and then I began to run, but the harder I ran, the slower I went. Finally I came to a halt, and the land folded beneath my feet and I suddenly found myself where I had been attempting to go.

The sky was overcast, clouds boiling. Thunder rocked the air, and lighting forked from cloud to cloud, creating a spiderweb of brilliant threads. Part of me wanted to reach up and touch one, to feel the current race through my body. The desire was so strong I almost brought Xan up into the air to attract the shimmering forks that danced scattershot through the clouds. But as I lifted up my sword, I realized what I was doing and quickly pulled myself back into check.

"You can't reach the sky," I told myself, even though right now it looked possible. I really didn't have a death wish. Riding the lightning wasn't my idea of the way I wanted to go out, and the urgency—the push—began to fade.

But that left the question of *Where was I?*

I turned around, trying to find something that would allow me to get my bearings.

To the north, dunes rolled by in an unending stretch of sands containing rogue magic—you could tell by the rust grains that sparkled among the mounds of pale yellow sand.

As I watched, a large mound at least fifteen feet high shook and twisted, rising to reveal a sand creature. Bipedal, its back curved, and like the

Sphinx, it was smooth and weathered, with no discernible features. It began to stride across the horizon, the ground shaking under the weight of its feet as it lumbered past me.

I watched it, unable to pull my gaze away. The creature was mesmerizing in its beauty, and yet, it could have crushed me with one finger. But it didn't even seem to notice me, and went on its way across the barren landscape until it disappeared into a dust devil that rose.

Fury? Fury, are you there? The voice echoed around me, caught on the wind, faint as if from a great distance away.

I turned, trying to discern what direction it was coming from before I answered. Tam had taught me to be cautious, to wait before answering, to consider the options. Perhaps it was a friend, but it could just as easily be an enemy.

Fury? I need to talk to you. Again, the voice rippled past. *I need to tell you something.*

And then, I was moving—swept along on a current of air that billowed up behind me. I stretched my arms out, reveling in the raging wind. It held me aloft like a skater held his partner, and I went gliding over the sands, my feet not touching the ground. The wind buoyed me up, twisting and spinning me as though I were an autumn leaf, and I spiraled up and then down, carried by the force. I laughed, feeling raw and wild and as I held out my hands to the side, globes of fire emerging from the palms, and I left a trail of flames in my wake.

I don't know how long I traveled, but after a time, the winds began lowering me to the sand again, and then, set me down. I was no longer in a desert, but in a rocky landscape, filled with twisted heaps of metal. And then I knew where I was. For the sculptures made no sense, angles intersecting in ways they should not. Curves turned into angles turned into fronds that feathered out like no metal ever should. The only place I had ever been that defied the laws of physics, logic, and gravity was the Tremble.

I was out on the Tremble, in an oasis of chaos.

The Tremble was to the land what the Broken were to humans. Whatever connection it had once had with the reality that we knew had long vanished, leaving in its place a surreal and terrifying landscape. Nothing was how it should be. Nothing stayed the same. Forever morphing and shifting, Gaia had left behind a garden of madness, a desert of desolation. Anyone who journeyed out on the Tremble for long risked losing their grasp on reality. None were spared.

When Tam had been cast out on the Tremble by the Devani—the enforcers who had been the Conglomerate's ruthless agents of order, but now who had vanished into the mists—Jason and I had gone after him. And we had learned just how powerful and brutal the Tremble could be. But we had also found allies who lived beneath the ground, safe from the ravages of the surface. And then—I knew.

I knew whose voice I had been hearing.

"Rasheya? Where are you? I hear you!"

The wind swept up my words, tumbling them away before they were even out of my mouth. I shivered, feeling stripped of my thoughts. There was no answer, save for the constant susurration of the breezes that continually swept past. I began to walk, wondering how I had come to be here. But the wind seemed to sweep away my thoughts as well, and I found myself wondering if I had really heard her calling.

A large statue of twisted metal rose in front of me and I gazed up at it, trying to figure out what it had been. It looped and curled in and around itself, with long tentacles of metal coiling off of the center core, and a large bulbous oval, dented and rusted, that must have at one time been a sphere in the center. I was still trying to puzzle it out when a long echoing scream rippled across the barren landscape.

A slow *swish-swish* sound alerted me and I whirled around. Behind me, walking toward me but showing no recognition, was a tall beautiful man wearing a gray duster and gray jeans. His boots looked to be soft leather, also gray, and over his back he wore a scabbard and sword. His hair was long, bound back into a ponytail, sparkling silver but it didn't look like it had aged that way. His face was angular and craggy, his cheekbones accentuated, and he kept his eyes straight ahead. They were the color of rich soil, with flecks of gold. It was then that I realized he was almost upon me. He had gone from being a great distance away to being right in front of me in the blink of an eye. But he didn't even seem to notice me, for which I was grateful.

I held my breath as he came face-to-face with me, but the next moment he was gone and I turned to see he had walked right through me. Shivering, I glanced over my shoulder to see four wolves, larger than any wolves I had ever seen, racing along the desert floor to catch up with him. They flanked his sides, and he didn't seem to notice them, but they kept the pace as though he were their leader.

There was something about him that terrified me, and I found myself praying that he would continue on his way, not noticing me. The next moment, I heard Rasheya crying again as a dark cloud began to form overhead. The man was gone, and I turned, trying to find Rasheya, but the land was gone. Everything had vanished except for the clouds around me. And all I could hear was, *He is coming.*

"FURY? FURY, WAKE up, love!"

I blinked, shaking my head as I realized I was under the covers, in my own bed. I pushed myself up, scooting so I was leaning back against the headboard. Tam was bending over me, a worried look in his eyes.

"Are you all right? I heard you crying." He stroked my face, scooting onto the bed beside me. "What is it, love? Did something frighten you?"

I nodded, trying to figure out what it happened. "I'm not sure if I had a dream or I was actually out of my body. But I was out on the Tremble and I kept hearing Rasheya calling for me. I was trying to find my way to her when I saw a tall man accompanied by wolves. He walked through me, and I don't think he saw me. But he was frightening, Tam. Something about him scared the hell out of me, and I don't know why."

"Did you recognize him? Do you think it was Lyon?"

Lyon had been the leader of the Order of the Black Mist, and he had placed a bounty on my head. Jason had helped me trap him out on the realm of Chaos, but whether he still lived or not, I didn't know. Jason had been trapped there as well, and it'd taken him months to find his way into Limbo, from where Hecate and I had rescued him.

"No," I said slowly. "I would have known Lyon by his energy, as well as his looks. This wasn't him. In fact, I didn't get the same sort of energy off of him at all. Lyon was crazypants scary. This man... There was a focus and determination about him that unnerved me. Something about his eyes—there was a danger in his eyes that looked deliberate."

"You should talk to one of our artists. See if they can draw a sketch of him. It couldn't hurt, although it may have just been a dream. Meanwhile, we have visitors from Seattle. I want you to come talk to them. They made a discovery that may make it worth a trip to the ghost city."

He kissed me gently, holding me for a moment until I felt safe and secure again. I tried to clear my head of the dream, although even in sleep, the Tremble left me feeling upside down and inside out.

"Take your bath and dress and have some breakfast. Meet me in the throne room in an hour." Tam kissed me again, then strode back out of the bedroom.

Patrice was waiting for me. She had filled the tub with warm soapy bubbles, and gratefully, I stepped into the water. I sank down, feeling chilled from my nightmare.

"What would you like to wear today, milady?"

"Apparently we're holding audience in the throne room, so it had better be something official. How about my Harvest dress?"

When we greeted new visitors coming into the village, I had acquiesced to Damh Varias's requests that I dress more formally. We had found an acceptable compromise. As long as I wore my crown, at other times I was free to wear jeans and whatever top I wanted. But for formal functions and greeting visitors, I dressed like the queen was expected to dress.

Patrice smiled, saying nothing as she went over to my wardrobe. She liked it when it was time to doll up, and I didn't blame her. It gave her more leeway to get creative with my makeup and clothing, and also, she was born to UnderBarrow. These formalities and traditions were part of her upbringing.

I scrubbed my skin with a sponge, leaning back to let the warm water soak into my muscles. The dream had bothered me more than I had let on, but I was well aware that sometimes, as Tam said, a dream was just a dream.

As soon as I finished bathing, Patrice toweled

me dry and held out my dress for me to step into. Made from a print of scattered harvest leaves against a pale background, the dress had a fitted bodice, and an attached waistband that tied in a bow in back. It had a low V neck, and a slit running up the right side so that I could grab my whip if need be.

"What shoes would you like, milady?"

I thought about it for a moment. "The black ankle boots with stiletto heels. The ones with silver buckles." She fetched them from my wardrobe and then guided my feet into them, zipping them up the side. Afterward, I took my place at the vanity and she set a plate of bread and cheese in front of me, along with a large mug filled with tea. As I ate my breakfast, she brushed my hair, braiding two thin braids, one to each side, then drew them back, fastening them around the rest of my hair with a silver barrette. She placed my crown on my head and then began handing me makeup as I quickly applied shadow and liner, mascara and lipstick. Finally, I straightened and stared at myself. The crown shimmered with jewels and silver.

"I suppose I'm about as ready as I'll ever be."

"Earrings? And how about a necklace?" She opened my jewel case.

I nodded. Might as well make a good impression. "The carnelian necklace, and the smoky quartz earrings."

Patrice draped the necklace over my head, cautiously skimming the crown. She then handed me the earrings and I slipped them through the holes in my ears.

"There, you look properly attired to receive an audience, milady."

There was a faint sense of scolding in her voice, and I pressed my lips together, trying not to smile. In some ways, Patrice was better suited for her station than I was for mine. But we got along well, and Tam liked her, and I had come to think of her as a friend.

Armed with her approval, I stood and waited while she opened the door and called for Zed and Elan. Following them, I headed down the hall, toward the throne room.

THE THRONE ROOM of UnderBarrow hadn't changed much since it had first been built, from what Tam told me. So large you couldn't see from one end to another, the ceiling was so high that it was out of sight at the top of the dome. The walls were illuminated with flickering lights that emanated from behind the crystal-like surfaces. Benches and tables had been artfully scattered around the chamber, never impeding sightlines to the throne, and no chair sat higher than either throne at the center of the room.

Our thrones had been carved out of black marble, every square inch etched with intricate carvings. Ivy and holly grew up around the thrones, trimmed back to allow access to the steps leading up to them. Around my throne, crimson roses grew as well, with wicked thorns that drew blood at the slightest touch. The backs of both thrones rose well overhead, and crystals that looked very much like icicles interspersed with silver spines to form a halo that stretched in a semi-circle over the top of both seats.

Tam was already seated on his throne, dressed in the colors of UnderBarrow. With his tumbling hair and his piercing gaze, he cut a fine figure and if I hadn't already been married to him, I would have fallen in love all over again.

Zed and Elan walked a step behind me, their hands on their blades, always prepared. As I approached my throne—which sat next to Tam's—he stood, waiting for me. I knelt briefly in front of him before he held out his hand and guided me as I ascended the stairs to my seat. I sat down and he followed.

Once I was seated, Tam looked over at me. "Are you ready, love?"

I situated myself, making sure I was comfortable.

"As ready as I ever am," I said, smiling.

The first couple years, learning how to greet and receive visitors with just the right balance of friendliness and regality had stymied me, but I had it down now, and the sense that I belonged in Tam's world had grown. Fewer complaints were heard about the "upstart queen," and Tam assured me in another twenty or thirty years, people would rail behind me, not because it was their duty, but out of love. I wasn't exactly betting against him, but I'd believe it when I saw it.

When we were properly situated, Tam signaled to Zed, who motioned to the Herald-in-Arms, whose job it was to announce everyone who entered the throne room for an audience. A side door opened and in walked a scruffy band of travelers. They had cleaned up, that much I could tell, but they looked weary and out of hope.

They approached the throne. There were five of them, two men, two women, and a teenaged girl. By their looks, I guessed they were a family. The older man and woman looked about the same age, and the younger woman looked a lot like them. The girl, however, looked like the younger man.

They knelt and I could almost hear their sighs.

"His Majesty, Lord Tam of UnderBarrow of the Winter Court, and Her Majesty, Lady Kaeleen the Fury of UnderBarrow of the Winter Court, may I present Elizabeth and Argent Kenner, their daughter Maribel and her husband Shaun, and their daughter, Trina. They have come from the ghost city."

They waited, still kneeling, till Tam leaned forward.

"You may rise."

As they stood, looking up at us, I could see the dust in their eyes, the wariness that seemed to be permanently affixed to their faces. I wondered how long they had been on the road, and how they had managed to survive in Seattle for the eight years since the city fell.

"What brings you to Willow Wood?" Tam asked, motioning to one of the servants. "Bring them something to sit on."

As soon as they were seated on a long bench, the man—Argent—spoke first.

"Your Majesty...Majesties, thank you for receiving us." He looked anything but grateful, but I attributed that to a hard journey. "We've come from Seattle, yes. We were living there but it's grown so dangerous that we finally decided to leave. But I have news for you, if you would let us stay here and see how we get on."

Bargaining. It was a common tactic. The exchange of information to secure a place to stay, for at least a few nights. We had seen many come through trying the same. Some we allowed to stay—for good or for a rest. Others we passed on, immediately escorting them outside of our borders. Those were usually the ones who felt dangerous or sketchy.

Tam stared at Argent for a moment, then he said, "We will hear what you have to say. You may stay on a trial basis for two weeks. If you get along and agree to the rules, then we'll see about adding you permanently to our village. If not, then we'll send you on your way with a few days' rations."

I trusted Tam's judgment. He was exceptionally good at reading people.

Argent took a deep breath and let it out slowly. I could hear the whistle of air from where I sat. It looked like a hundred pounds just fell off his shoulders.

"Thank you. We appreciate it. I'm leery of traveling through the woods, and none of us know how to fight effectively."

That I didn't believe, but shook it off. We heard

the same from just about anybody who had come to stay. They didn't want us to know they could fight, probably out of self-preservation. But it didn't matter. If they messed up, we had the guards to take care of them.

"What information do you bring us, then?"

Argent nodded to Elizabeth, who gave him a firm smile. She turned to us.

"We were on our way out of Seattle when a group of zombies attacked us. We hid in a staircase that led into a basement. It must have belonged to an old pharmacy, because there was a treasure trove of medications there. Bandages, pills, liquids, just about everything you could want for. I had a padlock with me, so when we managed to escape, I locked the door and marked it with my symbol. It's on the northern side, near the Tremble. I can't guarantee anybody else hasn't found it, but it's in a heavily infested part of the city so I doubt many people are looking around there."

I blinked. We could stand to stockpile medical supplies, especially as we were still trying to get our hospital up and running. The healers had worked overtime on developing enough salves and tinctures and powders to cope with the most common afflictions, but we were still a ways from feeling secure in our ability to treat a number of conditions.

But I had learned. I didn't display any feelings one way or another, simply nodded to her and asked, "You say the zombie hordes are still running through the city?"

Elizabeth nodded, shuddering. "It's bad. Disease

is rampant. For those who live, there aren't any medics or health clinics to go to. So if somebody catches something infectious, it will spread. The ghosts are thick, and they manifest day and night. And at night, the ghouls come out in packs. Bog-dogs have bred themselves silly, and are found in all parts of the city now. I gather down by the actual Bogs it's even worse." She paused, then added, "You might as well know now—you'll find out soon enough. My granddaughter is a Theosian."

My gaze flickered to the girl. The teen looked just as weary as the adults, if not worse. In her eyes I saw despair, and that she was so young and feeling so hopeless made my heart ache.

"Are you bound to a god?" I asked.

She shook her head. "No, I was supposed to go before the gods when I was five, but the tsunami came and the world changed."

I glanced at her mother, Maribel. "You realize if you stay, you'll be required to submit her to Gudarheim for testing, to discover which god she's to be bound with? I'm Theosian. I'm bound to Hecate."

Maribel, the mother of the teenager, nodded. "That's why we came here. Before Seattle fell, I heard of you. *Fury, the Abomination chaser.* When we learned that you were ruling over Willow Wood, we decided to come here. There are a number of people blaming the Theosians for causing the second World Shift, and we were afraid of ending up in a place where they might try to take her from us and..." She stopped, biting her tongue as she held my gaze.

I could read the unspoken words on her face. If people were blaming Theosians for the World Shift, chances were they'd be looking for a sacrificial goat. And a young teen not bound to any god or goddess yet made an easy target and an even easier victim.

Turning to Tam, I whispered, "Call Jeffie. She can take them to clean up and rest, and ask her to set up an appointment for them at Gudarheim for the girl."

He nodded. "Yes, they need food and rest and some peace."

Straightening up, Tam motioned to Zed. "Call for Jeffie."

He turned to our visitors. "We'll provide you lodgings where you can rest and eat. We'll contact the gods who are living near UnderBarrow and they will send for your daughter and test her. Rest your fears for now. You are safe here. But," he said sternly, leaning forward again. "Make sure you follow the rules. Do not break them. We are friendly and generous to our people and our guests, but one step over the line—especially deliberate—and we won't hesitate to send you packing. Understand?"

It sounded harsh, but the world was a harsh place and growing more so, and we had dealt with would-be upstarts in the past who had tried to test our patience and our hospitality.

But if our guests took offense, they showed no sign. Argent simply bowed his head and said, "As you will, Your Majesty. We'll do our best to fit in and mind our manners."

Zed returned with Jeffie, a lovely Fae woman who looked like a summer maid, but fought like a seasoned warrior. She led them out, chatting with them brightly. As soon as they were gone, Tam motioned to Zed.

"Is there anything urgent on the calendar today? If nothing requires immediate attention, we'll dismiss court and meet you in the Council Chambers."

Zed shook his head. "No, Your Majesty. A few cases, but they aren't immediate."

"Then summon Damh Varias and the Sea-Council to meet in the Blue room in an hour's time. Her Majesty and I will be there in a while." Tam rose, and held out his hand to me. As I took it, standing, the guards left in the room knelt. Followed by Elan and a couple of the other guards, we headed back to our chambers, remaining silent until we were behind closed doors.

As Elan left, shutting the door behind us, I turned to Tam.

"What do you think? Is it worth a trip to Seattle? We could use the supplies. We're badly in need of some of the things we still haven't managed to formulate yet."

We had lost several patients due to our inability to process certain medications and treatments. So much had been interwoven with the big corporations who manufactured necessities of life. We could grow our own food and make our own tools and clothing, but there were some things that required functioning technology, and the techno-mages hadn't been able to figure out how to compensate for those things yet. Open heart surgery was once again a dangerous procedure, though Tam's healers were helping the medics who had joined us from Seattle to learn new ways of operating.

"I don't like the idea of going. The city has fallen so far, so fast, that I consider it more dangerous than the Tremble." Tam paced the length of the room, looking grave. "I won't argue that we don't need those supplies, but at what cost? We haven't been to Seattle in over a year and the last time we lost two people."

He was right on that count. The last time we sent a scouting expedition to Seattle, they had come home broken and bruised, missing two of the party. Unfortunately, there was no chance of rescuing the two who were left behind. They had gone down under a horde of zombies and if they hadn't been lost in a carnivorous binge, they would have been turned. But if we went in knowing exactly what we were facing, it might actually be worth the chance.

"Last time, we just sent a regular salvage party." I sat down at the table, leaning on my elbows as I thought it through. "What if we went in fully prepared?"

"Fully prepared as in how?" Tam cocked his head.

"Remember when we first arrived here? We went back there for a major salvage and Thor took us in his chariot. What better way to return than to do that again? If Thor were to accompany us, we'd all be much safer. We could take warriors.

The last scouting party we sent was made up of a small group of salvage hunters with a few guards. Plus, this time, we'd go in knowing what we were looking for and where the supplies were, so we wouldn't have to worry about hunting around the city. If we go fully armed and convince Thor to go with us, I think we stand a damn good chance of coming out of it unscathed. Also, since the ghouls are running in packs, we go in at dawn and get out before dusk." I was getting more excited by the moment. "It would work. I know it."

Tam worried his lip. "It makes sense. But you said 'we.' Surely you aren't thinking of going?"

I knew I had an argument ahead of me. "Listen. I know I'm the queen, but I'm also the best Abomination hunter out there. And chances are, in addition to the zombies and ghouls, Seattle's overrun with Aboms since I haven't been down there to stop them for the past eight years. They're going to need for me to come along." I paused, then added, "Besides, I want to see... I had a dream about the Tremble last night."

"Oh no, you're *not* going to the Tremble!" Tam's eyes flashed. "I will not allow it."

I twisted my lips, wondering how much to fight him on this. I didn't think he was going to budge but merely said, "Let's wait till the Sea-Council meets and see what they think."

He sputtered, but then moodily shrugged off the conversation when Zed entered the room again.

"Your Majesties, we have more visitors." The look on his face alarmed me.

"What's wrong?"

"It's...Tigra, Your Majesty. Tigra and a few of her party have returned from their journey. They're back."

I stared at him. *Tigra* was back? After five years, she had returned. Tam sat down beside me, looking as astonished as I felt.

"Show her in, please," I said, hoping that the answers to a lot of our questions would be laid to rest now that the weretiger had returned home.

Chapter 4

TIGRA WAS A weretiger. Before the second World Shift, she had worked as a member of Lightning Strikes, a multi-governmental organization aimed at monitoring the weather for any indications of magical meddling.

After the tsunami had wiped out Seattle, she had set off with a group of explorers to find out exactly what was left of the American Corporatocracy. As the years passed and we heard no word from them, I had reluctantly assumed they had been waylaid and killed. I liked Tigra and had tried not to dwell on the idea that she was gone forever. Her brother Carson lived in UnderBarrow, working with the techno-mages.

I slowly stood up, pressing my hand to my stomach. What would she be like now, after all this time? What would she have found out there?

"I'll bring them in after they've had a chance to

clean up. But the other members of the council are here." Zed opened the door to usher them in. Other than Tam, Elan, and me, the Sea-Council consisted of Jason, Laren, Elan's twin brother; Hans and Greta; Kendall, a Theosian pledged to Athena; Tyrell, a Theosian bound to the Dagda; and Sarinka, a healer. Damh Varias joined us, as well.

As they entered the room and took their places, Jason was looking gloomy. He went into periods where he was withdrawn and quiet. Elan and I both knew it was from his time lost in the realm of Chaos, but he wasn't always easy to deal with during these times. As the years passed, though, he seemed to experience them less and less and I hoped that one day they'd fully go away. His hair was drawn back in a neat braid now, and he was neatly dressed, so at least it wasn't bad. He took a chair next to Elan.

When everybody was in place, Zed closed the door behind him, and we were alone.

Tam motioned to me.

"We have two big items on the agenda today," I said. "First, we've procured information about a large store of medical supplies in Seattle. We have the location, and there's a pretty good chance that they're still untouched." I told them about our visitors and what they had said.

"So, we have to decide whether to mount a salvage operation. I vote yes, that we ask Thor if he'll take us in his chariot like he did once before. We go heavily armed, and we make certain to get our asses out of the city before dusk. While the zombies will still be a problem, that would curtail our chances of running into any ghouls." I turned to Hans. "What do you think he would say if we asked?"

Hans arched his eyebrows, then shrugged. He was a Theosian, bound to Thor, and had recently become a priest of the thunder god. "I think he might go for it. He's pretty easygoing and he likes mortals. And offering him the chance to crush a few zombies? Thor's a god of battle as well as agriculture. He might well be spoiling for a good fight."

"All right. What about the rest of you? What say you?"

Jason stared at the table. "Do you know these people are telling the truth? What if they're making it all up?"

"Then we come back with nothing." I shook my head. "And we kick them out. Why would they lie, though, knowing that they wouldn't be allowed to stay?"

Again, Jason shrugged. "What if this is a setup? A trap?"

I blinked. That thought had never occurred to me. "Lyon's long gone into the realm of Chaos. The Order of the Black Mist has disbanded, as far as we know. Who would have a grudge against us except for him?"

Elan cleared her throat. "I agree with Fury on that count. My father might begrudge us success, but he isn't stupid enough to break the alliance that our villages have. As far as anybody else... well...there *isn't* anybody else. Not in any organized fashion. And the zombies can't rationalize, or even really think."

"I was just suggesting a possibility. But fine, if you choose not to follow up on it." Jason looked cross, but he kept his voice soft, and went back to staring at the table. I wondered what the hell was up.

"What about you two?" I motioned to Tyrell and Kendall. We had met them during our journeys, and they had joined Willow Wood, given there was nothing to return to in Seattle.

"I think we should go for it," Tyrell said, his voice booming. He was a massive man, looking more like a warrior than a healer and bard. "The Lady Brighid was mentioning the other day that the healers are skilled but some things are beyond even their ability without the proper herbs and equipment. I'm willing to go, and I'm no slouch when it comes to fighting off zombies."

"I concur with Tyrell. The winters are only getting rougher, and as the years go on, we can only rely on ourselves. If there are stockpiles that will help us stretch out our medical supplies for a few years, that provides yet another leg up on rebuilding our lives here. We've come a long way, thanks to you and Lord Tam, but we can't ignore anything that can give us an edge." Kendall placed her blade on the table. "I'll add my blade to the salvage party."

"I agree with them." I turned to Tam. "This could be a huge boost to our stores, and it would make it easier on the healers. That will give us more time to plant our own herbs and weave bandages and everything else that our medical care entails. We have power for the hospital, but without the proper supplies, that does little good."

He held my gaze for a moment, and I could feel the concern and the love hiding behind those liquid silver eyes. Then he nodded. "Very well. We'll stage a salvage party to Seattle."

"I'm going." I did not phrase it as a question. "There will be Aboms over there. Queet and I will be going, as long as Thor agrees to lead the charge." I turned to Hans. "Perhaps you could approach him?"

Hans nodded, thrusting his hands in his pockets. "Yeah, I will. I'm not sure what he'll think, but I don't expect an outright rejection."

Zed tapped on the door again, peeking inside. "Your Majesties, they're ready."

I nodded. "Give us five minutes, then show them in." Turning back to the others, I added, "Tigra and her party have returned."

Jason let out a gasp. "They're alive?"

"Apparently so. Zed's bringing them in now." I worried my lip. "We haven't seen them in six years. I'm thrilled they're back, but walk softly. We don't know what might have gone on during that time." I hated being suspicious, but we didn't have the luxury of trusting they would be who they were when they left. They had been gone for years, and we had no clue of what had happened in the intervening time. I wanted to celebrate, but it was best to wait and see exactly what we were dealing with.

Zed returned, followed by four people. Eight had set out, if I remembered correctly. Tigra's brother had stayed behind with us, but she and seven others had headed off to explore what was left of our country, if anything.

Tigra Inashki had left here five-ten and a sturdy one hundred and fifty pounds of muscle. Now, as she entered the room, she looked gaunt. Her pale golden skin with faint black chevrons was criss-crossed with scars and a haunted look filled her honey-colored eyes. Her gorgeous hair, once long, was still the same gold with black highlights, but it was short now, cut into a rough shag.

She knelt in front of Tam and me, followed by the three men who looked vaguely familiar. They all looked rough, though, as though they had been on the road a long time without a reprieve. As I motioned for her to stand, she caught my gaze. She reminded me of a wounded animal, the look in her eyes cut so deep.

"Fury. Your Majesty," she added quickly.

"Bring them chairs, Zed. Have you had a chance to eat?"

Tigra nodded. "They fed us when we came in. It was the first real meal we've had in days, but we don't dare eat more. Not till the food settles in our stomachs."

We waited until they sat.

Tigra motioned to her party. "You remember Luke, Juan, and Merritt, right?"

I nodded, even though in truth, I had forgotten their names. But they came back to me when she introduced them. "You left with eight in your party."

She grimaced and nodded once. "Yes, we did. The other four fell along the way. The world has grown harsh, Your Majesty—"

"Fury, in private," I said.

"Thank you. *Fury*. When we left, we intended to journey to Atlantea, to see if the Devani were gathering there, as we had heard. We never made it there. The panic and damage was so widespread that we were lucky to get as far as we did. We headed southeast, intending to skirt the Texicana Gulf, but when we headed down the Baha-Cali Coast, we ran into trouble. The quakes had destroyed so much of the land, it took us weeks to navigate through the devastation. The crevasses and fissures run deep down there. We finally gave up and headed east."

Knowing what the Seattle area had looked like after the quakes and tsunami, I could imagine just how bad it had been elsewhere.

"What did you find?" Hans asked. "Were there many people alive?"

"Dead bodies everywhere. The survivors began to band together. We found numerous small villages...and too many nomad packs. We lost Winston somewhere along that first leg of the journey." She stifled what sounded like a sob. "We ran into a group of nomads who were searching for food. Apparently, they lost their discrimination in what—or who—they hunted. They took Winston down. I don't think I have to tell you what his fate was."

I closed my eyes, not wanting to even think about it. All I could hope for was that he had died painlessly.

"We spent months working our way into what we think were the Mid-Lands and the Prairie District. The damage was mostly to the cities there. The land was relatively unscathed, but the cities had fallen. There, people were more civilized. We stayed in several villages for weeks at a time to rest up. We traded work for room and board. But what happened here, happened there as well. The zombies came in off *all* of the World Trees, so what was left of Lyon's group had managed to strike across the country. And the survivors banded together, fortifying the villages they built against the undead."

"What about the Devani?" Tam asked.

"No sign of them anywhere. That's why we were determined to make it to Atlantea, to find out what we could. But by the second winter, we were lost. We had no clue where we were, and all the maps in the world weren't of any help. We spent... I suppose it was months hiking around, trying to find our way to civilization. We ran across a lot of dead bodies. Some zombies here and there. We lost Sheryl to quicksand. We couldn't get her out before it sucked her down. Finally, shortly before our third winter, we realized that we had gotten turned around. We were in the foothills of the Rocky Mountains. By then, we knew we weren't going to make it to Atlantea, so we set out to come back. But the mountains are difficult to travel through. Some days, I doubt we managed five miles. The roads had degraded so that they weren't much help, and there were creatures in the hills. They must have come in off the World Tree because I *never* remember seeing anything like them. Large, ugly brutes that lurk in the rocky climes. They don't look human at all, or anything quite like it."

"How did you lose the other two?" Jason asked.

Tigra shrugged. "William fell when we were trying to scale a tall cliff. There was no getting around it so we *had* to go over. He slipped off the rope. And Arlene was caught by a large mountain lion. She had shifted into her dog form and couldn't fight it off when it suddenly appeared from behind a rock.

"Finally, we found our way back here. We stopped in Verdanya and asked if Willow Wood still stood. They weren't all that friendly but gave us some food and let us rest for a bit. We traveled from well before dawn to get here."

They had spent six years on the road, and all that they had to show for it were four dead companions, and proof that the country had fallen. We truly were on our own.

"But you saw no Devani anywhere?"

Tigra shook her head. "Maybe they went back to their realm. Or maybe they do hold Atlantea. But not once on our trip did we see one of the golden warriors."

There was speculation that the golden-skinned warriors turned goon squad for the Corporatocracy had actually been aliens, biding their time till they could make a grab for control. But the second World Shift had thrown a monkey wrench in their plans. Even if they did hold Atlantea, right now that meant very little, given what Tigra had just said.

"I'm glad you're back. Are you going to stay?" I asked.

She nodded. "Yeah, I think I'm done journeying. I want to settle down, just live quietly for a while." Pausing, she added, "My brother? Is he still here? Is he all right?"

"He is," Tam said. "Carson is actually working with our techno-mages on creating useful contraptions to help us weather this shift. They're working on a computer that runs via magic, which would make me happy as all get out. I miss my technology." Tam had been the techno-geek for Dream Wardens, long before Jason or I knew he was also the Lord of UnderBarrow. He had managed to keep that fact to himself.

"Zed will take you to your brother when we're done here, and Sarinka will give you thorough checkups to make certain you're healthy. I want all of you to rest for a few months before you even start to think in terms of what you want to do. You've earned it." I reached out to tuck Tigra's hair behind her ear. She looked so different than when I first met her. She had been pulled together, strong and vibrant. Now, she looked worn.

She hung her head. "I tried. We tried so hard. But the country's like a giant maze now. So little remains of the bigger cities. I imagine the entire world has been through this. All the great cities have probably fallen."

"Cities rise, and they fall, as do civilizations," Tam said. "I've seen them come and go for thousands of years. And they will continue to do so, long after we're gone. But we persevere because it's all we can do."

Nodding, Tigra wiped her eyes. "That they do,

Tam. That they do."

And with that, Zed led them out, and shut the door behind them.

I turned to the others. "Well, we have an answer of sorts. The nation is gone. We're on our own. I suggest we fortify our defenses, strengthen our alliances, and raid Seattle for what's left."

"I concur. There's no cavalry coming to rescue us. If you want to lead the charge, my love, then so be it." Tam lifted my hand, kissing the top of it, his lips barely brushing my skin.

I shivered. So much of our affection was kept to our private chambers that even a simple touch from him could set me off. "Tomorrow morning, then, if Thor agrees to go. I won't chance it without him." I turned to Hans. "Will you go now and ask?"

He nodded. "I'll head over to Gudarheim now." He excused himself and left the room."

"Kendall and Tyrell will go, and of course, Hans. Who else?" I turned to the others.

"I will," Greta said. "Freya will let me take the time, I'm sure."

"And I, of course," Elan said.

But Jason surprised me. He cleared his throat. "I'll go, too."

I caught his gaze. "Don't you need to stay with Aila?"

He shook his head. "She'll be fine with Laren."

Laren, Elan's twin brother, was more of a thinker than a fighter, though he could swing a mean sword. But he wasn't currently fit for a raiding party, having broken his wrist not three weeks before when he fell off his horse.

"I'll take care of her," Laren said. "No worries there."

"What about the shop?" I wanted to ask him if he thought he could manage the trip without panicking, but I wasn't about to embarrass him in front of everyone else. But his willingness to go surprised me and I couldn't help but wonder what was behind it.

He merely shrugged. "I can shut up Dream Wardens for a few days. I might be able to find some supplies I need while we're over there."

I frowned, then nodded. "Very well. Sarinka, you need to stay here, but can you work us up a first-aid kit to take with us?"

"Of course, milady. I'll have a page bring it over to you this afternoon." The healer curtseyed and left.

Tam couldn't go, of course. Unless we were directly going into war, it went against custom for the Lord of UnderBarrow to go into a dangerous mission. Technically, I shouldn't be going either, but I was actually chafing to go see what we could find and Tam knew it. He indulged my need for adventure as often as he could.

"Then we have our crew. We'll take Zed and three other guards. I think we should all be able to fit in Thor's chariot. That is, if he'll take us there." Never assume anything about the gods. That was the first lesson I had learned as a Theosian.

As we adjourned the meeting, Tam caught my attention. "I'd like to see you in our private chambers, if you would."

I caught the nuance in his voice and suppressed

a smile. "Of course."

As we headed back to our chambers, with Elan accompanying us, I decided to confront the elephant in the room.

"Do you think Jason can manage a trip like this? Honestly?"

She grimaced. "I can't give you a good answer. If he thinks he can, then perhaps he's ready. But I'm not sure what spurred on his desire to volunteer. I don't think he's in favor of the raid, but for some reason, he's decided to come along."

"He's been depressed lately, I've noticed."

"The moods hit him. Being lost in Chaos, and then Limbo changed his brain chemistry. He's never fully been himself since that, but most of the time he can manage the moods. So I'm not sure. Maybe he wants to shake it off. Shake off the past, by going to confront the past?" She frowned. "I'll talk to him tonight. If I have the slightest glimmer that he won't be able to manage the journey, I'll tell you and you can order him to stay back."

I nodded, glancing at Tam. Ordering Jason to do anything would put a rift in our relationship, whether it was Tam or me who did it. But we couldn't risk the entire party to take one questionable link along.

When we reached our chambers, we excused Elan and entered the suite of rooms. Patrice was there, waiting. I glanced at the clock. We were running on close to noon.

"We'll call for lunch when we're ready. After you help me out of this dress, you may leave us and I'll ring for you in a while." I paused, then added,

"Tigra's returned. Please go find Dame Ferrika and ask her to find a temporary maid for her. She needs some looking after, I think."

Patrice dropped into a curtsey. "Yes, milady. I'll return when you summon me." But as she helped me out of the dress, hanging it up neatly, I could see the smile lurking on her face. She took off my boots, then brought me a dressing gown.

As I slid into the blue silk robe, I waved her off.

As soon as the door closed, Tam locked it behind her. Then, he turned to me and held out his hands. "I want to see you," he said, his voice husky.

I dropped the gown, letting it slide from my shoulders to the floor. Beneath it, I was wearing a thin pair of panties and a demi-bra. I reached around, unhooking it and tossing it on the bench to my vanity. Then, shimmying out of my panties, I turned, naked, and felt the warmth of the fire grow between my legs.

Tam motioned for me to cross to him. He took me in his arms, pulling me against him. The feel of his hands against my skin made me moan and I closed my eyes, breathing in his fragrance. He smelled like the fresh breath of autumn, with cinnamon and cloves and the scent of apple, and when he held me close, all my cares fell away. Tam was my safety net, and yet his passion ran deep and fierce. His lips met mine, and he held the back of my head, his fingers lacing through my hair. His kiss ran deep, from my lips to my clit, stirring my fire and waking me up. Every inch of my skin tingled as he ran his other hand over my back and down to cup my butt, squeezing just hard enough to tell me that I was his.

I moaned in his mouth, wrapping my arms around his neck as I pressed my breasts against his chest. The material of his tunic was rough against my nipples, abrasive, and yet the feel of the embroidered threads intensified my arousal.

"I want to feel your skin. Undress," I whispered, pulling away from him.

His gaze locked with mine, he stepped back and slid off his tunic, dropping it to the side. He pointed to his jeans, to the belt that encircled his waist.

"Unzip me," he said, the order abrupt, taunting me to obey him. We played this game well, switching sides as the mood hit us.

"What will you do to me if I obey?" I ran my fingers down my breasts, pinching my nipples and gasping from the sudden jolt. Then I slipped the fingers of one hand between my lips, licking them, then trailed my hand down toward my mound, finding my target. I began to circle my clit lightly, all the while staring into Tam's eyes.

"I'll fuck every inch of you. I'll eat you out until you beg me to stop, you wanton wench of mine." He pointed toward his jeans. "Unzip me. Suck me dry, woman."

I shuddered as he spoke. I knew so well just how skilled of a lover he was. He never let me forget that my pleasure always came first to him. And yet, when he was forceful and demanding it gave me a chance to let go, to release my responsibilities, to simply attend to his pleasures and forget every other care.

As I knelt in front of him, once again it hit me

how long Tam had lived, and how much he had seen. I felt dwarfed in front of him, though he never tried to make me feel that way. I reached for his belt and unbuckled it, then slowly drew down his zipper. Pushing his jeans down, I caught my breath as he sprang up, full at attention, thick and hard and throbbing. He had the perfect cock, the perfect girth, and as I knelt in front of him, I wanted nothing more than to take him in my mouth.

I slipped my lips over the tip of his shaft, closing them so that the head had to push them open, to slide through the suction I created. Tam let out a loud moan and braced himself, holding onto two chairs as I began to work him hard. I slid his shaft into my mouth, relaxing my throat as I took in as much of him as I could fit, then slid back. Once again, I pressed forward, licking and nibbling as I worked him in my mouth, and then I picked up the pace, bobbing my head against him as he began to thrust.

"Harder," Tam gasped, letting go of the chairs and leaning forward to hold the back of my head. He thrust himself into my mouth and. I began to suck hard, and cupped his balls in my hand, giving them a gentle squeeze.

"Do that again," he ordered, and I obeyed.

"I'm going to come," Tam said, tensing.

I gave one final lick and he came in my mouth. I swallowed the salty fluid, feeling it race down my throat. But before I could lean back, he reached down and lifted me to my feet. He placed his hands on my shoulders and walked me backward toward the bed, his gaze locked onto mine.

"How do you want it?" he growled.

I caught my breath. "I want to ride you."

A delighted smile upticking the corner of his lips, he swung around me, then languidly stretched out on his back, stroking his cock. "Am I your stallion?"

"You're my everything," I said, climbing across the massive bed on my hands and knees. I straddled his pelvis, then leaned forward to kiss him, my tongue tasting his, my breasts rubbing against his chest. He reached down to finger me, stroking me as I stroked his chest with mine.

Looking up at me, he whispered, "You are so beautiful. My Fury. My fire. I'm your moth, circling your flaming spirit."

I rose up, cupping my breasts. "Taste me."

He slid down between my legs till he was beneath my sex. I lowered myself as he leaned up, his tongue tasting me, swirling in circles. The hunger within me grew, my desire spreading through me like a vining plant, tendrils seeking out every nerve, every trigger to send me soaring. I closed my eyes, my breath heavy, as he continued to stroke and lick me, nipping me with his teeth at one point so that I screamed, but the scream was grounded in pleasure as well as pain, and the echo of it was lost into the corners of the room.

I leaned down, crawling backward, and he took my breast in his mouth, sucking hard, nipping just hard enough to send me into another paroxysm of desire. My body burning with hunger, I once again straddled his pelvis and lowered myself onto his shaft, driving down with a slow, deliberate speed.

His girth parted the lips of my vaj and I groaned as he thrust upward, holding tight to my waist, filling me deep and spreading me wide. I paused, focusing on the feel of him inside me, then began to move, swirling my hips as I rose and fell on his cock, my sex slick from my growing need.

And then, he rolled me over, moving between my legs, grinding deep, looming over me with those luminous eyes, his gaze drilling deep into my core. I cried as he moved inside me, feeling all the boundaries between us fall. The walls tumbled down and there was only Tam and me, only our love and our passion and the undying promise of our life together.

"Fury, never leave me. You're my queen. You're my goddess."

I began to cry. "Love me. Just love me forever."

And in the sudden hush between us, I came so hard it hurt, and after he kissed me, Tam went on loving me through the long autumn afternoon.

Chapter 5

THE NEXT MORNING we gathered outside of UnderBarrow. Thor had agreed to take us in his chariot, and we were making ready to leave. I gazed at Tam and for a moment, my heart wavered. I didn't want to leave him, but I knew that I needed to go.

Hecate was standing beside Thor, talking to him in low whispers. I wasn't sure what they were discussing, but she had insisted on attending the meeting when she found out I planned on going.

I turned to the others. We were geared up, ready for travel. Zed, Wheel, Fortune, and Shawna were with us. I had thought of taking Len, but I didn't want Shevron to worry even more. She was standing back, watching the proceedings, her gaze fixed on her brother. I wandered over to her.

"You know he volunteered, right? I didn't order him to go." I didn't want her thinking that I would compromise her brother's mental health. Shevron had helped Jason take care of me growing up, subbing for the mother I had lost. And finally, she had forgiven me for leaving him behind in the realm of Chaos, and also for encouraging her son to enter the Guard. But push a mother bear too many times and eventually she'd strike back.

"I know." She crossed her arms, watching him. "I wish you could order him to stay behind, but I know that he has to go. I don't know why, but he has to go with you."

"Are you afraid he won't be able to handle it?" I paused as she cast a veiled look my way. "If you think it would endanger either him or the rest of us, tell me."

Shevron was as tall as her brother, and so pale she kept out of the sun as much as possible. Her hair was lighter than his—a shimmering platinum—and her eyes were brilliant blue. She sighed, then shook her head.

"I don't know, to be honest, Fury. I don't know *what's* going on. Last night it was like he had taken some sort of upper. He was so hyper I was worried about him. Even Aila noticed. She asked me—in private—why her daddy was acting so strangely. Elan and I discussed it but she hasn't a clue either, and when he's in a mood, prodding him about what he's feeling isn't the best choice. He's never turned violent—in fact, I don't think he has a violent bone in his body. But he can blow up like nobody's business, and I get worried he might turn his anger on himself." She let out a slow breath. "He's never been right, not since..."

"Since he was lost in Chaos. You can say it." I had long given up defending myself for my choice. It had been either leave Jason, or risk the Elder Gods of Chaos breaking through the World Tree. I had made the only choice I could.

She nodded. "Yes. I wonder what he saw out there that scrambled him so much."

I hesitated, then said, "Maybe it isn't what he saw, but the confusion that comes with that realm. When we were on the Tremble, it was much the same, I think. Stay out there long and you go mad. Everything moves and changes, nothing stands still and there are times when what you see makes no sense. Even though we were only there a few days, I still remember the confusion."

Shevron turned to me. "I blamed you for so long, and I know you think I still do. But I finally understand. I've had a long time to think about it. You didn't have a choice."

"No, I didn't," I said. "It was leave your brother, or risk the world. I made the only decision I could."

"Well, then. I guess there's no way to know what would have happened if he hadn't been trapped there." Shevron scooted closer to me. "Fury, keep an eye on him. I don't trust this sudden desire of his to go with you. He's barely wanted to leave his home or shop for the past eight years. Something's happening and I'm not sure what."

I placed my hand on her shoulder. "I will. I promise." Then, seeing Tam motioning to me, I added, "I have to go now. But Shevron, remember that Jason is a grown man. He makes his own choices. I could forbid him from coming, but…I think maybe he's trying to step outside the cocoon he's made for himself."

"I get it," she said, then waved me on.

I headed over to Thor and Hecate, who were standing with Tam.

A steady, persistent drizzle misted down on us, and the ground was wet but not yet muddy. I shivered, my legs catching a draft that passed by. I hadn't put on my cloak yet, mostly because I knew that once we were inside Thor's chariot, I was planning on just leaning back, draping it over me like a blanket, and snoozing.

"So, Thor tells me that he's outfitted his chariot with a little more comfortable interior," Tam said, sliding an arm around my shoulder. Damh Varias gave him a dark look, but Tam ignored him. Even this was too much of a display, according to the Bonny Fae traditions, but given I was headed out on a dangerous mission, I ignored Damh Varias's look as well.

"Really?" I turned to the thunder god.

He was a hulk of a man, nearly seven feet tall. His *muscles* had grown muscles, and his shockingly blond hair spilled down his back. His beard was copper, and he wore snug jeans, a muscle shirt, and a leather jacket decked out with a massive amount of hardware. He also carried Mjölnir, a hammer that was—for all intents and purposes—more weapon than any of us ever really needed.

Thor laughed. He was a good-natured sort, especially considering he was a god. He was eating a roast beef sandwich, the scent sharp with the tang of mustard, and the aroma set my mouth to watering even though I had already eaten a perfectly respectable breakfast.

"Yes, indeed. Since the lot of you went to sleep the last time we traveled, I fiddled around with my chariot and put in some cushions and blankets. Also spare water jugs and pound cake. You can never have enough pound cake."

Thor had developed a taste for lemon poppy seed pound cake. Shevron had confided in me that she sent at least three pound cakes a day to his office.

"Cushions are good," I said absently. Then, turning to Hecate, I said, "Can we have a brief chat before I leave? I want to ask something. Also, where's Queet?"

Right here, Fury. Queet's voice echoed on the breeze. We used whisper-speak, which few others could even hear. He whipped around me, buoyed up by the breeze, and whirled as a fall of leaves came flying past.

You're excited, aren't you? Admit it!

Yes, all right, I'm excited. It's been awfully quiet lately and I haven't had much to do.

Hecate had assigned Queet to me when I was young. My spirit guide and I hadn't always gotten along, and he had been downright surly part of the time, but he was always there when I needed him, and he always had my back. However, since we had settled in at Willow Wood, he had become positively sedate.

Hecate walked me over to a bench where we sat on the edge, trying to keep from getting our asses soaked by the puddles of rainwater. She reached out and took my hand.

"This is a dangerous mission. You have been training regularly, but you haven't been out on the road for a long time. Are you sure about this?"

I considered her words. She wasn't soft on me like Tam. If she expressed concern, there was a reason. After a moment, I answered.

"Yes, I'm certain. There's a reason I have to go. Even Jason's going and you know that he would never have volunteered if he didn't think it was important. Well, I mean since..." I paused. Hecate had helped me bring him off the plane of Limbo, but it had been a harrowing experience and one I didn't like thinking about.

"Yes, I know. Do you think what Tigra said made a difference in how you're viewing life now?" Hecate always knew exactly what questions to ask.

I nodded. "Definitely. The realization that we're truly on our own hit home. I suppose I've been wondering if we were just a pocket of the world cut off from civilization, but now I know that *we are* civilization. Unless there's a miracle out there, this is as good as it gets. So we've got to start from here if we want to work our way up. Gaia didn't leave much, did she?"

"She left far more than she did the first time. But remember, if humans hadn't forgotten—or ignored—her decrees, if Lyon and the corporations hadn't gotten greedy, and if the artifacts from the Weather Wars had been destroyed instead of being hidden away in a foolish idea to use them one day, none of this would be happening. This wasn't

Gaia's first choice."

"I realize that," I said, choosing my words carefully. "I wasn't blaming her, but Hecate, she did unleash the tsunami."

"No, she just helped it along. The quakes Lyon set off unleashed it. But none of that matters now. The only thing that matters is that it not happen again. Anyway, I want you to be cautious. You're no longer just Fury, the Abomination fighter. You're a queen, and you have a kingdom to look after."

I squeezed her hand, smiling at her. "I'm first and always yours, Hecate. I'm bound to you, and I have never, ever regretted that. I'm bound to your will. What you would have me do, I will do." Even as I said it, a very small part of me prayed she'd never ask me to leave Tam. That would be the ultimate test of loyalty.

"I know that. I'll never ask you to do anything that isn't absolutely necessary," she said, as if reading my mind. "But I do ask you to be cautious. And whatever you do, don't forget about the lycanthrope attack. It goes far deeper than a few rogue mutants. I don't know all the facts, but there are rumors on the wind—and they do not bode well."

"Will you tell me what they are?" Forewarned was forearmed.

"No, because they are simply that as of now. Rumors. And it never does well to let unchecked speculation make the rounds. I don't wish to add confusion to the picture. Or to cloud your judgment. You may come across the truth quicker than I can, and I don't want anything I say to obscure actual fact from gossip. So go, but be careful, and don't tarry too long in the city of ghosts. It's never good to walk among the dead too long, or to breathe in the stench of decay. And that is all Seattle is anymore—a memory cloaked in decomposition and pain."

She walked me back to Thor's chariot where the others were waiting. I crossed to Tam and slid into his arms for a good-bye kiss. The hell with decorum. I wasn't leaving without his arms around me, and without meeting his lips with my own.

"Be careful, love. Come back to me." He leaned his forehead against mine.

"We'll take care of her, Your Majesty," Elan said, standing at attention.

"I know you will," Tam said.

Thor motioned for us to gather 'round. His chariot was a thing of beauty. Hooked up to his two goats—Tanngrisnir and Tanngnióstr—it was the size of a large van, at least on the outside. Rich cherry red in color with bronze accents and wheels, Thor's chariot could carry up to fifty people inside. Or a whole lot of goodies.

The two goats, who were as immortal as their owner, were capable of returning to life each time they were killed, and Thor had roasted them many times over. Our first winter here, they had fed a number of people each night as we struggled to sustain ourselves.

"I want to stop at Wyfair," I said before entering the chariot. "I want to ask if the Frostlings have heard anything of the lycanthrope attacks."

"Will do." Thor motioned for me to enter the

chariot.

I ducked my head, bending over to step into the enclosed chassis of the vehicle. Zed followed behind me, then Hans and the others. We settled ourselves on the new cushions, and I slid my cape over me like a blanket. Thor was right, the inside of the chariot was far more comfortable. It was a magical space. I had my suspicions that we were in some sort of tiny dimension that was only accessed via the thunder god's chariot, but I had never asked. Once we were going, though, we traveled fast and furious, though it felt like the gentle rocking of a boat from inside.

Thor peeked in the door. "Ready?"

We nodded. If we had forgotten anything, it was too late to get it now.

He slammed the door, and Jason cast a light spell so that we could see. A moment later, the chariot began to move.

I leaned back against one of the cushions. Travel in the chariot made me sleepy for some reason, though I wasn't sure why. Maybe it was the sensation of rocking. Maybe it was the inactivity, in an enclosed space. Maybe it was just that I never seemed to get quite enough sleep. Whatever the case, I leaned against Elan's shoulder and closed my eyes. Within minutes, I was fast asleep.

"FURY, FURY? WAKE up. Thor's slowing

down."

I blinked, yawning as I sat up and stretched. My head had somehow landed in Elan's lap, and my feet were on Jason's lap. I squinted in the dim light and gratefully accepted the water bottle that Zed handed me. I took a long drink then wiped my mouth, handing it back.

"How long was I out?"

"Who knows. We never have been able to figure out time inside of Thor's chariot," Jason said with a laugh. "I suppose we're approaching Wyfair, unless something else has put a halt to our journey."

Wyfair was the village of the Frostlings. The creatures had come into being long ago, the product of a marriage between the ancient Fae and ice elementals. However they managed to merge their bloodlines, they were both powerful and mystical, and they lived a step outside of our world, while still maintaining their place in it. The Frostlings made me feel like a dust speck on a kitten's nose.

A moment later, the chariot pulled to a stop and Thor opened the doors.

"We've reached Wyfair. Something's wrong, Fury. You're going to want to see this. All of you." Thor sounded worried, and when a god was worried, it was never a good sign.

We crept out of the chariot and I saw we were on the outskirts of the village. Hidden within the woods, the city was created out of what looked like ice, but over the years I had come to realize that the material was actually a form of crystal—shatterproof and as solid as the rocks from which it was mined. The buildings weren't see-through, but more mirror-like, reflecting those who passed by.

Wyfair was a small village, and many who passed right by it never saw it. The Frostlings had a way of disappearing from the radar screen when they wanted to. But now, there was a stillness to the village that made me stop. Though the Frostlings moved silently, there had always been the feeling of life to them—a vibrant, magical feel that quivered in the air. But now? There was only the sound of the wind in the trees, of the birds singing their rain-songs in the surrounding forest.

I glanced over at Thor. "I can feel it. What's going on?"

"I don't know. I thought I'd fetch you all out here before we go in. Better forearmed than taken by surprise."

Nodding, I rested my hand against my leg, on my whip. I had never drawn a weapon in the village, and I was hesitant to go in armed, but if Thor felt there was something wrong, we needed to be prepared. I turned to the others.

"Be ready with your weapons, but *don't* show them until we find out what's going on. The Frostlings are very testy about such things. Understand?"

A chorus of "Yes" followed. Satisfied we were as ready as we could be, I motioned for Hans to go in front with Thor. Elan and I would follow, then Greta and Kendall. After them, Tyrell and Jason would follow, and then the guards.

Thor and Hans set foot into the borders of the village and Hans let out a gasp.

"What's wrong?"

"There's...no way to describe this. There's magic at work here, but I have no clue what kind." Hans looked at Thor. "What do you think?"

Thor hesitated. "I have felt this before, long ago. In a battle. I can't recall which one—there were so many, but I remember this feeling. Sorcery runs deep here."

"Not Lyon?" I asked, praying we weren't dealing with the Order of the Black Mist again.

"No, this is no magic from humankind, whether Theosian or pure mortal." Thor jerked around, staring intently at a swath of bushes. "I could have sworn..."

Hans drew his sword. "We'd better arm up. Be careful, Your Majesty."

I slapped my thigh and my whip came off in my hand, glowing and crackling. As I stepped over the boundary line demarcating the entry to the village, instantly, I could feel what they were talking about. Wyfair felt haunted. It felt abandoned—no, I thought, not abandoned. But...in stasis. As if everything had suddenly come to a halt.

It was then that I caught sight of one of the Frostlings. He was beautiful, looking carved out of the ice fields themselves. His face was smooth, as was his body, but the energy around him whispered "male" and so I knew it was a "he." But he wasn't moving. He stood frozen, staring at something in his hand.

I walked over, carefully, but making enough noise that he should have heard me. Instead, he remained silent as the grave, immobilized. Hesitantly, I reached out and tapped him on the arm, but even then, he neither spoke nor moved. Worried, I tried to see what was in his hand, but whatever it was seemed to have vanished.

"What's going on?" I turned to Hans, who quickly advanced to my side.

"I have no clue. But he seems to be unaware of us."

"He seems to be unaware of *everything*. What—" I stopped as Zed shouted something from across the street. He was standing by another building, peeking in.

As he jogged over to my side, we all gathered around.

"Your Majesty, there are more of the Frostlings inside the building, all frozen. They look like they were right in the middle of everyday activity when whatever it was—happened. The whole village seems to be caught in some sort of magical stasis."

Slowly, I nodded. "Stasis" was right. They weren't dead—or if they were, it was unlike any death I'd ever seen. They didn't even look hurt. Then again, I had no clue what an injury to a Frostling would look like or whether they showed any response to pain.

"Fan out, check the rest of the village, and hurry. We don't know if whatever is affecting them can affect us, too. We don't want to get caught if it can. In fact, Elan, Jason, Zed, you three come with me outside of the village borders. Thor, would you keep an eye on the others? Search the village as quickly as you can for anything that looks out of the ordinary."

I hustled my ass back over the border, breathing

easier as the heavy pall fell away and it once again felt like we were in the woodland. I leaned against Thor's chariot, contemplating what might have happened. Speculation wasn't an answer, but at least it might give us possibilities to consider.

"Ideas? I'm open."

Zed glanced over his shoulder. "Who can use magic that strong?"

"Given all the world has been through in the past eight years, I don't even think we can begin to answer that question. Jason, you're a mage. Tell me, how powerful would you have to be to cast a spell to freeze an entire village?"

Jason's depression seemed to have vanished. He was staring at the village, his face lit up with curiosity. Jason was a thinker. Give him a problem to solve and he'd dig into it like a bog-dog and hold on until he mastered it.

"Honestly, there are few who could manage it, at least out of the mages I've known. I can't be sure, of course, but a spell that powerful would be beyond most of the sorcerers that I've ever met. I don't know if it's an actual paralysis spell, or whether it's a stasis spell. Whatever it is, you would have to have a buttload of experience to cast it. You'd have to be far older and more experienced than I am, that's for sure."

At that moment, there was a shout from the other side of the village. Wheel came racing back, a look of dread on his face.

"I found... I found..." He paused, leaning over with his hands on his knees, trying to catch his breath.

"Take it easy, but tell us. Is an enemy on the way?" I craned my neck, attempting to see if anybody was approaching, but all I could see were Thor and the others still poking around the village.

"No—I don't know. But I found a couple bodies on the other side of the village. They're torn to bits, like the ones in the campground." He winced as he straightened.

"Frostlings?" I couldn't imagine lycanthropes being able to take down a Frostling.

"No," he said as he stretched. "No, I think they're human and I'm guessing there were three of them, though it's kind of hard to tell."

Thor and Hans were headed in that direction. I wanted to yell at them to be careful, but they knew all the precautions and wouldn't do anything rash.

I rubbed my head, feeling a headache creep toward me. "The lycanthropes can't have developed magic this powerful. They're too chaotic to handle it. They can't have done this."

"I concur," Zed said. "They're many things but they aren't magically inclined. And even if they were, I doubt if they'd have the dedication and genius to pull off this sort of spell."

We waited until Thor and Hans returned. Thor was carrying a large, bloodstained bundle and I had the horrible feeling I knew exactly what was in there. He lay it down gently by the chariot and silently pulled a shovel out of the cabin.

"We bury the dead," he said. "I'd pyre them but we don't have the luxury of time to stick around to make certain the forest doesn't catch fire."

"Lycanthrope attack?" I asked.

He nodded. "Most likely. We found prints. There aren't many creatures who leave such distinctive marks when they run. I'm not sure who these people were, but..."

"Zed, you and the other guards had better have a look at them. See if you can recognize who they are, so perhaps we can find the next of kin." I didn't like ordering my men to look upon the face of horror, and maimed and mutilated bodies were definitely that, but on the off chance Zed or the other guards had seen these people, I wanted to be able to tell their families. Not knowing was the worst thing of all. I'd been through it several times and it was never easy.

Finally, everyone gathered back by the chariot. Elan was looking queasy.

"I recognized them, Your Majesty. They're from Verdanya. They're scouts, for the king. No doubt they were attempting to woo the Alezakai into some sort of trade deal or something of the sort. We'll have to notify my..." She paused, then said, "We'll have to notify the king."

"We'll do that as soon as we get back to Willow Wood. For now, bury them."

Elan presided over the interment. We couldn't do much, but Thor made quick work of digging the graves, and Elan stood witness. Then, without a clue of what to do about the Frostlings, we gathered back in the chariot and set off again.

BY NIGHT WE had come to the land bridge leading over to Green Lake. We made camp beside the narrow strip of land that crossed the junction where the Horned Owl Inlet met the Wild Wave Inlet. Thor started a merry fire and offered to roast a goat for us, but we had brought supplies for a few days. I liked goat, but I was in the mood for bread and cheese and apples. I toasted a piece of bread over the fire, then held the cheese in the flames till it began to melt, and smeared it across the bread. As I bit into it, the taste of the mellow, golden cheese hit my mouth, followed by the crunch of the toast, and I sighed in pleasure.

I was sitting beside Hans, Thor, Greta, Elan, and Jason. The guards sat apart from us, ever watchful even as they ate. We were under the cover of a band of trees, but close enough to what was left of the road that we could be seen by passersby. I had been leery of going any farther into the woods given there were bands of lycanthropes wandering around, though we had come quite a distance from Wyfair and there was no hint that they had been through here. But neither had we come this way in a long time, and for all we knew, they could have started their own village along the road.

"What are you thinking about?" Jason asked me, handing me an apple.

I took it, polishing it on my cloak. "Lycanthropes. The world and how far we are from where we started. You've seen more change. You're a lot older than I am, but in thirty-eight years, I feel like I've lived three lifetimes over. The first with my mother, the second with you and Shevron after Marlene was killed, and the third, when the world blew up again."

He nodded, staring at his hands. "You'll get used to it. I feel that way too, though compared to someone like Tam, I'm a babe in arms. Everything cycles. Everything has its time."

I hesitated for a moment, then asked, "Jason, why did you come? I'm not sorry you're here, but..."

"But why did I take a chance on my mental health and venture out?" He glanced at me.

I nodded. "I suppose you can put it that way. Your sister is worried about you, you know. She talked to me before we left."

"And Elan, no doubt, is worried as well." He let out a soft breath. "I think I'm ready to rejoin the land of the living. Being stuck out on the realm of Chaos broke me, in some ways. I've never felt completely whole since then. My daughter deserves a father who isn't afraid of his own shadow. Aila is so...vibrant. So filled with life. But I notice she'll defer, pull back when I'm around. I think she senses my conflict and she doesn't want to make it worse. I won't have her growing up having to stifle who she is out of fear it will hurt me or make me feel bad."

"So you've decided to face the hordes? Scare yourself awake, so to speak?" I cocked my head, holding his gaze. "It takes a brave man to admit he needs help, and an even braver one to face his own fears for the good of another. Do this for yourself, though. You deserve to spend the rest of your life free from your fears and memories." I held my hands out closer to the fire.

"I did blame you, a little. I can tell you that now. I know you made the only choice you could. I told you to go. I told you to leave me. But...I think a little part of me thought I was more important than the rest of the world. So I blamed you. But a few years back, I realized just how selfish that was. I don't blame you anymore."

Jason took one of my hands, holding it lightly. At one time, that act would have set off a host of longing in me. After Jason took me in, I had developed a puppy-love crush on him, but he never returned the feelings. Oh, he loved me, but he never could love me the way I had hoped. When I gave up the dream of Jason, reality had hit in the form of Tam.

"I'm glad you don't blame me. I understand why you would—it tore me up to leave you there. But it's over and done and Lyon is, I hope, forever lost in the realm with the Elder Gods he loves so much." I squeezed his fingers. "And you have Elan and Aila. And I have Tam. And we have a life, even if it's not the one we envisioned a decade ago."

"In some ways it's better," he said. "The government was corrupt. Society was rocky and becoming more precarious. Now, we rely on ourselves and we make the rules. You're a good queen, Kae. You and Tam...you belong together."

"We do." I winked at him. "We should get some sleep now. Morning will come early and we've got a ways to go, though I'm sure Thor's chariot will get us there in one piece."

As we stood, ready to crawl back inside the chariot to sleep while Thor kept watch, there was a rustle from the nearby bushes. By the light of the fire, I caught sight of a glint of tooth and fang as a band of lycanthropes burst out of the woods, pouncing on us before we could draw our weapons.

Chapter 6

THEY CAME OUT of nowhere, surrounding our camp. There were at least twelve of them, running on all fours as they surrounded us in a semi-circle, snarling and snapping with their jagged teeth. Their muzzles were disfigured, an odd cross between human and wolf, and a dangerous light gleamed in their eyes as they jockeyed for position while trying to avoid the fire. They carried no weapons, but with their teeth and sharp claws, they didn't really need them.

I slapped my thigh, my whip coming off in my hand. As I raised it, the leather began to spark and flame, and I moved away from the others so as not to accidentally strike them.

Elan and the guards were immediately en pointe, drawing their weapons and spreading out in front of me. Behind me, Jason let out a shout. Hans and Greta strode forward, their swords out.

And Thor... Thor strode forward, Mjölnir in hand.

The lycanthropes froze as he came into view. Whether they knew he was a god, I wasn't sure, but they eyed him warily. Then one of the lycanthropes let out another snarl and leaped forward to tackle Wheel, who met the attack with raised sword.

I wanted to be in the thick of it, but if I moved to join the guards, they would focus on making sure I didn't get hurt, and that would endanger them. So I waited, whip ready in case the creatures should break through.

Thor began to jog, whirling his hammer over his head. He let it fly as he cleared the fire. Mjölnir went whirling toward two of the lycanthropes, taking them down as it skidded along the ground, knocking them over like bowling pins. The creatures whimpered, one letting out a shriek, as blood spattered from the impact.

The other lycanthropes paused as the great hammer rose and flew back to Thor's hand. Unfortunately, so did the guards. Wheel's opponent took advantage of his hesitation, launching himself onto the guard and knocking him to the ground. I was about to race to his side when Elan leapt into a whirling kick, managing to kick him square in the side of the head, sending him reeling sideways. Wheel scrambled off the ground.

Greta and Hans had engaged another of the creatures, and between them, they were dodging his claws while taking turns attacking. Their blades were hitting true, but lycanthropes were tough. Even though the creature was bleeding from numerous slashes they had managed to land, he was still on his feet, though he seemed to be slowing.

Elan plunged her sword through Wheel's attacker, square in its heart. When it collapsed onto the ground, she smoothly withdrew her blade and turned to survey the rest of the camp.

Fortune and Shawna were tackling another lycanthrope, following Greta and Hans's lead. Tyrell had backed away, drawing glowing glyphs in the air for a spell of some sort, while Kendall protected him, engaging one of the creatures who headed their way.

Behind me, Jason was stripping, and the next moment, he flew over the camp in his hawk form, shrieking as he swept down to attack another one of the creatures, landing a blow to its face with his talons.

I was champing at the bit, wanting to fight, when a rustling from behind startled me. I whirled to see that one of the lycanthropes had taken the opportunity to sneak around and now it was coming directly at me. I raised my whip and began to swirl it overhead, the flames sparking as it turned. Just before the lycanthrope reached me, rearing up on his hind legs, I let the whip fly, bringing it down to slash across the creature's face and body. It drew a neat line from his nose down across his stomach, the flames igniting his fur and leaving a deep gash in its wake. Apparently, I had put so much oomph into it that I sliced open his abdomen. I grimaced when I realized I had managed to eviscerate him. His internal organs steamed in the night air as they slithered to the ground. The lycanthrope looked down as though he wasn't sure of what had just happened, then clutched his stomach and toppled over.

I backed away, waiting to see if another had followed him, but there were no more in sight. When I turned to see how the others were doing, I did so just in time to see vines creeping out from the forest, grabbing hold of two more of the lycanthropes. The vines were glowing, and Tyrell was holding out his hands, aiming directly toward the tendrils. The vines appeared to be tightening, constricting the creatures so they couldn't move. Kendall darted forward, stabbing each through their hearts as they were held helpless.

Thor had sent his hammer at one of the two remaining beasts, and Elan and Wheel took on the last. In his hawk form, Jason had managed to blind his opponent, and Shawna darted over to finish him off. Another moment and we were done, standing in the middle of the bloody encampment.

I slowly lowered my whip, easing back toward the chariot. "Are there any more, do you think?"

Thor held up his hand for silence. He closed his eyes, and then, after a moment, he shook his head. "I don't hear any nearby. But there's a smell…" He bent down to sniff one of the dead lycanthropes. "I know that scent. I've smelled it before." He paused, then shrugged. "It will come to me. Meanwhile, everybody get in the chariot and I'll stand guard till morning."

"Are you all right, Your Majesty?" Zed said, eyeing me closely.

"Yes, I'm fine. Startled and worried, that's all." I glanced around the group. "Did anybody get hurt?

And where's Jason?"

Just as I asked, a great hawk came swooping down next to the fire, and a moment later, Jason stood there, nude and looking shaken. Elan silently handed him his clothes and he quickly slid into them. Everybody was fine, minus a scratch or two, but it was obvious that if Thor hadn't been here, we would have been toast.

"What do we do about their bodies? They'll attract other scavengers," Elan asked.

"Never mind. I'll take care of it. Into my chariot."

Thor hurried us inside and then closed the door. Jason cast a light spell, but none of us were very talkative and we soon bundled under the blankets. I was grateful for the cushions. I wasn't fond of sleeping on the ground under drizzly skies.

As I bedded down, wishing Tam were by my side, I thought I heard a shout from outside, but then all was quiet and I closed my eyes, certain I wouldn't be able to sleep. But my body proved me wrong, and the next thing I knew, it was morning and Thor was waking us up.

"UP AND AT 'em," Thor said, opening the door. "It's a nippy morning, so bundle up."

As we tumbled out of the chariot, the encampment looked calm and collected. There was no sign of the bodies anywhere, and a merry fire was crackling with a pot of cereal cooking over it. I grinned. It still astonished me when the gods took part in mundane tasks like cooking or cleaning, but I had come to learn a lot in the past eight years of living in such close proximity to them. The gods were a lot like us, only more powerful, and usually a bit wiser.

I shivered as I gathered my cloak around my shoulders. My shorts left my legs bare, and that meant cool autumn air on shivering skin. I had brought my leather jacket but was saving that for when we were in Seattle proper, where I'd have to be on high alert and able to move easily and quickly. Wearing a cloak protected me from the chill, but it wasn't quite so easy to dart around in, or to free my whip.

Elan pressed a cup of hot brew in my hands. The Norse gods had given us something else—a nonalcoholic drink that tasted a lot like coffee, had a live-wire kick to it, but was easy to grow in our climate. They called it *vaknop*, which they said meant something akin to "wake up." And wake you up it did.

I took a long sip of it, closing my eyes with pleasure as the hot, slightly spicy, liquid flowed down my throat. Instantly, I felt more alert and warmer. As Fortune began to ladle out bowls of the cereal, I carried mine over to a fallen log and sat down next to Hans and Greta.

"Last night was worrisome." I set my mug down on the ground as I began to eat.

"I had worried about the pack of the creatures who attacked the foragers, but this attack means there must be more than one pack on the hunt. We know lycanthropes roam the woods, but they aren't all that common and that we have several packs hunting is, yes, quite worrisome." Greta shook her head. "The winters are getting colder and longer, have you noticed? There wasn't frost this morning, but it won't be long before we find it at our doorstep."

"Gaia cooled the planet during the first World Shift. I'm beginning to think she did so again this time." Hans spooned his cereal into his mouth, catching a bit in his beard.

Greta leaned over and wiped it off for him and I couldn't help but smile. They had grown into their marriage, and while Greta had told me she'd never have children, being a Valkyrie, she also told me they had talked about fostering a child. Tam was promoting the practice. He said it encouraged the village to come together, to band as a united group rather than just a town.

"Do you think that has anything to do with the lycanthropes?" I couldn't see the connection.

Hans shrugged. "Honestly, I don't know, except they do seem to thrive out in the woods better than they ever did in the city. They had to live beneath the ground there. Remember, they can breed, and out here, they have the space to claim territories. Even as we've claimed our boundaries for Willow Wood and UnderBarrow, the lycanthropes may be intent on growing their population and staking out territory, which normally wouldn't be an issue. Except for one problem: they hunt anything and everything. And they seem to do well in cooler climes."

"If the world is cooling, and they thrive in colder climates, then we've got a long-range problem on our hands." I motioned for Elan and Jason to join us. Thor followed them over.

"Hans thinks the lycanthropes may be branching out in the woods, trying to expand their population."

Jason frowned. "But the one problem with that is they've never banded together before. Oh, they did to a small extent in the Underground, but more often than not, they are so territorial they're practically solitary."

"Then *something* must be uniting them. And that begs the question of what or who is bringing them together?"

The thought of the lycanthropes banding together under a common banner scared the hell out of me. They were tough enough individually, but if they joined forces, they would be a formidable force. We would be hard put if they decided to wage war on the village. And given Tigra's information, we couldn't expect help from anyone else. Everybody seemed on their own.

"Last night, the bodies smelled funny. I was trying to place the scent. I've smelled it before, and it's related to the feeling I felt at the Frostlings' village." Thor paused, closing his eyes for a moment. "For a moment, I thought maybe Loki was back, but even though the scent reminds me of him, it's not quite the same." He shook his head again. "No, I can't recall. There have been so many battles, and so many enemies over the years. It will come back when it's time. Are you ready?"

I nodded. "We should get moving." I looked up at the overcast skies just as they burst open and a deluge of rain broke loose. Pulling my hood over my head, I headed for the chariot as Wheel began to gather the dishes and put out the fire.

Within minutes, we were underway again, heading over the land bridge into the Green Lake district. But it wasn't long before Thor stopped and opened the chariot again.

"You need to come out. We've been stopped." He didn't look particularly worried, so it couldn't be an attack, I thought.

"What's up?" I asked as I stepped outside, into a steady downpour.

We had crossed to the other side of the land bridge, only to find a gate barricading the entrance to the Green Lake area. Guards lined the gate, dressed in curious uniforms that looked ragtag and thrown together, but they were all wearing dark green and purple, and they were carrying swords.

Stepping up beside Thor, we advanced toward the gate, with Zed and Elan behind us.

From the midst of the guards stepped a tall man. He was wearing a leather jacket and leather pants, and around his head, he wore what looked like a leather headband with metal spikes on it. He was carrying a sword and wore what looked like a fine mesh chain tunic beneath his jacket. For some reason, he looked familiar, but I couldn't place him.

He looked at Thor and said, "Who are you and what do you want?" He sounded like he was clenching his jaw and I could see he had a couple missing teeth.

Hans stepped forward. "May I present Her Majesty, Queen Kaeleen the Fury of UnderBarrow, and Thor, Lord of Thunder."

The man blinked, cocking his head. "*UnderBarrow*? Didn't that used to be down in the Sandspit?"

I nodded. "Yes, but Lord Tam, my husband and King of UnderBarrow, moved it before the tsunami hit. Might I ask your name?"

For a moment, I thought he was going to order us to turn around, but then he seemed to relax. "I'm Karl Shefford, the sheriff of the Green Lake district." He scanned the rest of our party. "I thought you might be coming to raid our goods. There are a lot of marauders out and about these days."

I nodded. "Easy mistake, and it's always better to make certain of who's passing through your borders. We need to get through to Seattle. We're not here to make trouble, just passing by. And if you have time, I'd like to sit down and discuss any news that might benefit us both."

It occurred to me that it would be a wise idea to find out if they were having lycanthrope issues, and if so, for how long. I also wanted to see if they had any information on any news coming out of the Tremble.

"Then follow me," he said.

We quickly found ourselves heading toward a large house just inside the borders of the Green Lake district. The mansion had obviously gone from upscale to being retrofitted to manage with present conditions.

"This is my house. Welcome and well met." Karl ushered us toward the gates.

I noticed the number of guards staged around the perimeter of the land, and I also noticed that any houses that must have been nearby had been torn down.

A barbed wire enclosure ringed the house, with yet more guards positioned around the perimeter. More guards watched from watchtowers that had been built out of red brick and wood. The barbed wire was three layers thick, and there were sharpened logs angled toward anybody making a run for the wire walls. Just how many enemies were they attempting to keep out?

The guard at the gate saluted as Karl approached, but gave us a sketchy look.

"They're all right. They've come on a peace mission. They're just passing through." Karl waved to the guard and he slowly opened the gate as we entered. Thor left the goats to stand guard over the chariot, along with Wheel, Fortune, and Shawna. Elan and Zed flanked me as we entered the house, with Thor at the front and the others in back.

Karl led us into the house. A number of the walls had been removed to make one large room, with a few down a back hall. A woman was in one corner, cooking over a wood stove. The smell of stew hit me hard, and my mouth watered, but as I glanced at Thor, he shook his head in a slight warning.

"You folks hungry or thirsty?" Karl asked.

I paused, then said, "No, thanks. We ate on the road, and we don't want to deprive you of any of your rations."

"Then have a seat over there around the table. I'll be back in a moment." He headed down the hall.

It occurred to me that Karl didn't seem to have any deputies, though the guards could be considered as such, I supposed. In fact, when I looked around, the only people I saw inside the house besides the woman cooking at the stove were guards. I leaned toward Thor.

"Don't you find the lack of other townsfolk odd? Karl seems to be running things on his own. Even in UnderBarrow, Tam and I have Damh Varias and other advisors."

He cast a careful look around the room, then gave me a sharp nod. "There are more things that are off than that, but this is not the place to discuss them. I suggest we keep the meeting short, and do not reveal much about Willow Wood or UnderBarrow."

I glanced up at him. The concern in his eyes had me more worried than his words. Perhaps we shouldn't have come back here with Karl, but then again, could we have passed through the Green Lake district without trouble if we had?

Karl returned with a drink in hand. It looked like beer, with a heady foam. "If you folks want a drink, please say so," he said as he swung a chair around, then straddled it, leaning against the back. "We have plenty."

He seemed more relaxed than he had a moment ago and I felt my alarms beginning to stand down. Maybe he had just been on edge for some reason.

"So, you're the queen of UnderBarrow." He

paused for a moment. "You're also a Theosian. I remember you from when Seattle still stood."

I blinked. "Have we met? I'm sorry, but…" I paused, thinking again that he looked all too familiar.

Karl laughed, then, sipping the beer and wiping the foam off his lip. "You did me a kindness one day. You gave me a cup of coffee. I was on the Monotrain. I told you my name was Gin, short for Gino. Which was the nickname they gave me back then. Probably because I used a lot of Ginotep."

And then it flooded back. I remembered. I had been on my way to work at Dream Wardens and I had stopped for coffee. On the Monotrain, I had met a homeless man, a drug-dazed bogey with a couple missing teeth. I had thought him high on Opish, but apparently Ginotep was his drug of choice—it was rougher than Opish, and easier to score on the cheap.

He had seemed sad, and had looked so longingly at my coffee that I gave it to him. As the memory drifted back, I stared at Karl. Yes, it was the same man, though he looked a long shot healthier and far stronger now. He still had the missing teeth, but his eyes were clear and he looked well-fed.

"I remember you. You lived at Evermore." The government shelters were harsh. They'd give out drugs for free, but no coffee and little food—the bare minimum for survival. They basically kept the Broken, *broken*. The memory seemed so far away and yet it had only been about ten years, if that.

"Yes, indeed. I did. When Seattle fell, they locked the shelter down. If you were inside, you were basically zombie food. Luckily, I was outside. I was looking for work up here in the Green Lake district the day the city fell. I never went back, so I wasn't there during the tsunami, either. I managed to find a house that had been deserted—this house—and moved in. The rest is history. I built a community here over the years and managed to rise to sheriff." He polished off the beer and set the glass on the table.

He was telling the truth, and yet he wasn't. That much I could sense. There were strands of truth woven through his story but there was more he wasn't saying, and that was the part that made me nervous.

"You did me a good deed, so I'll do you one now. We don't let many folk pass through here unattended, but you can go through without trouble. I'll tell my men to let you pass. But I suggest you find another way home," he said, eyeing me closely. "Also, a word of warning. Watch out for lycanthropes. We've had a real problem with them over the past month or so." Karl frowned. "We fought off a raiding party two days ago. They headed west over the land bridge. We lost three men."

"I think we met them," Thor said. "They won't bother you again—at least that particular party." He cracked his knuckles and snorted. I realized it was a show, but it was a good one because Karl eyed him steadily, looking slightly alarmed.

"You killed them?" Karl asked.

"That we did, with only a few scratches on our part." Thor cleared his throat. "We should be on our way. Thank you for the warning. We'll find another way home without treading through your lands." He stood, straightening his shoulders and stretching in an impressive show of brawn. He picked up Mjölnir and tossed it in the air, spinning it once and then catching it as though it weighed nothing.

Once again, Karl grimaced. "Then be safe and may you find what you're looking for. But the ghost city is deadly. Watch your step. The entire area is tainted with decay and death."

Karl guided us to the door where he, along with two men who easily looked as dangerous as he did, guided us back to the chariot. As soon as we could, we were off, skirting the edge of the Green Lake district toward the point where bridges had once connected across to Seattle.

There were a couple ferries there now—one large and one small. We paid the ferryman the fare for the larger one, and he and his crew began to row us, along with the chariot, across what had once been called the Locks. The trip was short, and it was less than an hour before we set foot on the other side.

I breathed a sigh of relief as we left Karl's lands behind. As the ferryman departed, rowing back over the lake, I turned to Thor.

"I can't believe he actually remembered me."

"We're lucky he did. A fortuitous chance, or I think we would have had a fight getting out of there."

"You think so, too? There's something about him that makes me nervous. Something I didn't feel the day I gave him the coffee."

"Living through disaster changes people. I think, in his case, it wasn't for the better. But I'll bet you he'll outlive a lot of others."

I nodded slowly. "I don't think that house of his was abandoned when he found it."

Thor shook his head. "Nor do I. I'm pretty sure the owners are dead and buried where they won't be found. We should pass the information about Green Lake onto Verdanya, and to Wyfair. I doubt if Karl would attempt to spread out toward our area—it would be a long hike—but on the chance that his head grows too big for his britches, we should be prepared."

"We should just destroy that land bridge," Jason said with a shake of the head. "It wouldn't be that difficult, and it would erect a difficult passage between them and us. If we want to visit the ghost city again, there are plenty of other options."

"That might not be a bad plan. Bring it up at the next Sea-Council. Meanwhile, thanks to Karl, we have a longer trip home, I fear. I don't relish the thought of going south through the Bogs. We don't even know if the road is still navigable." We hadn't been that way in a long time, and I had no doubt the Bogs had grown even more wild and the passage more dangerous. Plus, that would take us right by the World Tree, and who knew what was coming off it now?

"We won't have to go through the Bogs." Thor stroked his long red beard. "We can contact Jerako—cross over to the Arbortariam. From there, it's not a bad jaunt back to Willow Wood. The Greenlings are our allies, so they will offer us safe passage."

"But can we find a ferry?"

The Arbortariam was an island across Wild Wave Inlet, inhabited by the Greenlings—beings devoted to Gaia who were much like trees, only sentient and mobile.

Thor frowned, then shrugged. "We'll figure it out. Come along."

We set out south on a broken stretch of freeway. There were no cars, other than the rusted heaps sitting on the sides of the road. The asphalt was in pieces, with plants thrusting their way through the cracks. The roads had buckled during the earthquakes, and the tsunami had done a number on what was left.

All along the sides of the road were strewn the ruins of houses and apartments and stores—now mostly rubble. Here and there a building still stood, weather worn and covered in Wandering Ivy. Other structures that had remained upright reeked of danger, precarious as they waited for an errant windstorm to topple them into the last stage of their lives.

We were approaching the turnoff to the Tremble. Part of me really wanted to venture out on the plain, to seek out Rasheya and find out whether she had truly been trying to contact me in the dream. But one look at Thor told me that I wasn't going to be able to cadge him into the side trip. I might be a queen, but he was a god, and his jaw was set in that way that told me not to even bother asking.

As we climbed into the chariot and headed along

the road, I leaned back against the metal and closed my eyes. We were all tense, especially after meeting Karl. I thought back to the lonely, lost soul I had met on the Monotrain. Now he was king of a domain that I knew, in the core of my soul, he had taken by force. That was what our world had come to. Maybe that was what it had always been.

"What's wrong, Kae?" Jason asked. He was sitting beside me, with Elan on my other side. He was cautious to avoid compromising Elan's position as one of the guards. He treated her like he did the others, with respect for her authority.

I shrugged. "I don't know. Meeting Karl left a bitter taste in my mouth. The man I remember was one of the Broken, but I didn't think—he didn't come off as dangerous. Now, I think he's killed more than his share of people who weren't out to harm him."

"Oh, he's seasoned in dealing out death," Elan said.

Queet, what do you think? I reached out, wondering if Queet was around or if he had taken off exploring. He could always find me—that wasn't a problem.

But there he was, right behind me, half-in, half-out of the chariot. On the spirit level, it didn't really matter.

Fury, the man is dangerous. I didn't want to mention this while you were there because I thought you might want to go looking for them, but he has a number of ghosts walking on his heels. A long line of spirits he's responsible for killing. Rest assured, he is a powerful man, and a

haunted one, and the combination can be deadly.
   Paranoid?
   Paranoid *doesn't begin to cover it. And he's not exactly wrong. He has the spirits of hundreds following him, out to take him into their realm. When you deal in death on such a mass scale, you'd better be prepared to spend your days haunted.*

Queet had spoken so softly in whisper-speak that no one else had heard him. I decided to relay the information, just in case something happened where I couldn't—or where I forgot—to tell Tam when we got home.

"He's a danger then, and greedy." Jason brushed his hair back from his face. He was looking less pensive than he had when we first started out. A little more like the old Jason, though I knew it couldn't be as simple as one trip to help sort him out.

"Yes, and yes." I wondered whether to tell them about the dream I'd had of Rasheya. Finally, I decided I'd better. "Not long ago, I had a dream that I was out on the Tremble. I dreamt that Rasheya was calling for me. She wanted to tell me about a man traveling through the land there, and how he was powerful and deadly."

"Karl?" Elan asked.

Jason shivered. When we'd been out on the Tremble, it had been a mind-altering experience. "If I never end up out on the Tremble again, it will be too soon. I managed it once, but after being in the realm of Chaos, it's a little too close to home."

It was then I realized that, even if I had convinced Thor to take a trip over to the Tremble, Jason couldn't have gone along. He would have been too fragile.

"No, it wasn't Karl. It was some other man. He had four wolves with him, and they flanked his sides as he crossed the Tremble. He terrified me, though I don't know why. I'm not certain what was so dangerous about him, but he was...chaos embodied. He owned everything around him. I know he's connected with the lycanthrope attacks lately—I just *know* it, though I can't tell you how."

Elan fell silent, pressing her lips together. Hans, who was sitting opposite to us, frowned. "Thor remembers the energy from one of his battles. You said wolves?"

I nodded. "He had four great wolves with him."

"Thor said it wasn't Loki. Odin, perhaps?"

"Odin's too busy at Gudarheim to bother with the Tremble. When we get back, I can remind Thor to ask about it. But we should be on our guard. Given the attacks, and then the state we found Wyfair in, something is definitely afoot." Hans scratched his head, about to say something else when the chariot stopped.

The door opened, and Thor peeked in.

"You'd better get out now. We have an issue, and I don't want you locked in the chariot in case things go down the wrong way."

As we emerged from the belly of the beast, I turned toward where Thor was looking and my stomach dropped. Dusk had fallen, and we were standing in the road, and up ahead was a great black carriage, pulled by four black stallions. Two men sat atop it, driving. Surrounding the carriage were at least twenty men, their eyes glowing with crimson light.

Vampires. And they didn't look like they had rolled in on the welcome wagon.

Chapter 7

"WANT TO MAKE a bet it's yet another old friend?" Jason whispered, standing beside me.

I immediately knew who he was talking about. *Kython.* Lord over the vampires in Seattle, he had originally been a Theosian, which settled the question of whether or not Theosians could be turned. And I owed him a debt. He had never called it in, and I had hoped he would forget.

One of the leathered guards headed over to the carriage and opened the door. Kython swung out, dropping lightly to the ground. He was beautiful, in a dark, magnetic way, with crimson eyes and jet black lips. He reminded me of Tam, given they both had a glaring intensity—they were hard to ignore, hard to even look away from. But Tam's charisma was bound up in passion, and in compassion where he deemed warranted. Kython's charisma was entangled with sheer power and the glamour all vampires possessed.

He was wearing a pair of black and white striped pants that made him seem even taller than he already was. He wore a black suit coat with tails, and beneath it, I glimpsed a cobalt blue shirt. His hands were sheathed in blue leather gloves. His raven hair flowed down to his butt like a waterfall, and atop his head was perched a top hat, black with brilliant blue feathers attached to the band. He was wearing platform leather boots that buckled all the way up to his knees. He had been carrying a riding crop the first time I met him; this time, he carried a scepter.

"If it isn't Miss Fury, the beloved of UnderBarrow, the voice of Hecate," he said, coming to a stop in front of me, his voice booming like an emcee. His men were all holding odd-looking weapons. I had no clue what they might be able to do, nor did I want to know. "You still owe me a favor, young one," he said, starting to reach for my face.

Beside me, Elan stiffened, her hand on her sword. On the other side, Hans did the same. They didn't draw their weapons, not yet. That would be a call to battle, and if we could possibly avoid it, we wanted no part in engaging a large group of vampires.

"That I do," I said, staring straight into those glowing eyes of his. "And I also remember you promised that it would be nothing against my ethics. But for now, if you're willing to let the favor stand, I'd appreciate it. We're here to raid a medicinal supply, if you'll let us pass through, and we want to get home as soon as possible."

He waited, then let out a short laugh. "I love how you aren't afraid of me, Miss Fury of the World Tree. *Hecate's voice*, even though now you smell like the Bonny Fae and the deep woods." He dropped his hand and crossed his arms. "I've taken over the entire NW Quarters. What gangs used to inhabit the area were killed in the famines, or by zombies or packs of roving ghouls. You'll want to be cautious," he added, glancing over his shoulders. "Night has a way of being deadly in the City of Ghosts. It used to be the bogeymen from the Junk Yard you had to watch out for. Now, they run like scared rabbits."

I realized that he had just given us an invaluable warning, even though we already knew some of it. And we were playing tit for tat. He had gifted me with information, and he would expect something in return.

"We were planning on camping before entering the city proper at daybreak. I had heard there were gangs of ghouls running around, as well as the zombie packs and other assorted delights." I paused, then slowly added, "I don't recommend going across to the Green Lake area. There's a trigger-happy sheriff over there who wouldn't take kindly to vampires invading his turf. We only made it through because he recognized me from a chance meeting in Seattle years ago. I don't think we'll get a second pass through his territory."

Kython cocked his head, staring at me for a long while. Then his lips crooked into a mischievous smile and he laughed. "Well, then, it's practically old home week for you. I'll take your warning under advisement. If you want to camp in safety, come with me and I'll put you up for the night. If you stay here, you'll be swarmed before long. It's dusk, and the hordes come out at night."

I caught my breath, wondering which was the safer route. The idea of being holed up in a nest of vampires wasn't exactly comforting, yet facing packs of ghouls and zombies before we even hit the city proper wasn't my idea of fun, either. Kython must have caught the indecision on my face because he laughed.

"Vampire's honor, you'll be safe. And your friends, even as tasty as you all look. Besides, it will give me a chance to reinforce my marker."

I suppressed a groan. Given I had made a promise to him, and that was as good as an oath, I didn't feel I had the wherewithal to refuse. I looked at the others, trying to ascertain whether they were getting the drift of the situation. I didn't want a bunch of dissent going on in front of Kython's group. But Elan and Jason both seemed to be waiting to take their cues from me, and even Thor was watching me.

Wording my answer carefully, I said, "We accept your offer of safe harbor for the night, and thank you for it. We will follow you to your quarters." If we were in the chariot, Thor could take off with all of us if it looked like a trap.

Kython winked at me, then raised his scepter. "These weary travelers are under my protection. Know that, and be damned should you violate my orders," he said in a loud voice that echoed through the empty streets around us. He paused, cocking his head again, though this time he looked like he was listening rather than curious, and then he motioned to the chariot. "I advise you get back in your vehicle. We must be off. I can hear the distant march of the ghouls, and they will be here shortly. Follow us, if you value your life."

And with that, we headed back to the chariot, and Thor shut us safely in. We began to move and I leaned back, wondering if I had just made a horrible mistake.

TWENTY MINUTES LATER, we were standing in front of an underground bunker. It wasn't the one I remembered from before, but more elaborate and decked out. Kython had made good use of the salvaged remains from the city. Thor stopped just outside the bunker to let us out.

I gazed at the heavily barricaded fortress—which was mostly underground—and at the heavy chain-link fence that had been triple-wrapped around the enclosure. In addition to three layers of ten-foot-high chain link, they had added a double layer of barbed wire. Bog-dogs, on heavy chains, were tied up around the gates and even though the creatures freaked me out, I felt rather sorry for them. I had no clue if they got off their chains much or were fed right, but neither was I inclined to inquire. They were dangerous, feral beasts and would eat me up even if I had a bag of bog-dog treats in hand.

The guards at the gates looked very much human, but they were burly and sullen looking, and I noticed that each one wore some sort of collar around his neck. They stared at us hungrily as we walked through the gates, though I had a feeling their eyes were solely on Elan, Kendall, Shawna, and me. I shuddered when, as we walked past the nearest, he reached out to grab my arm. His fingers hadn't even made contact before one of the vamps immediately sprang on him, slamming him to the ground, snarling with fangs down as he loomed over him. The guard began to cry and Kython laughed.

"Oh, my toys, my toys. They do test the boundaries now and then but I guarantee that none will be allowed to so much as touch a hair on your fiery head, *Queen* Fury. Nor any of your other companions. You are safe here." He snapped his fingers. "Take care of *that*."

I heard a crunch and glanced back in time to see the vamp who had thrown the guard down wrench his neck to the side, breaking it as quickly and smoothly as I broke a breadstick. Shivering, I averted my eyes, saying nothing. Elan, who was walking beside me, unobtrusively felt for my hand and I took her fingers in mine, holding tight.

We continued on to the double doors on the side of the building. One story high, it looked more like a stone bunker than a palace. Guards by the door swept it open, bowing as Kython sauntered through. The other vamps followed him, with us in their midst. I had taken the time to count them as we paraded forward. Kython had met us with a contingency of fifteen vampires. They were all men. I wondered what he did with the women he turned.

The bunker was lit by fires in sconces on the walls. There was plenty of light, though it was the soft orange of fire rather than the illuminated colors of the faerie lights in UnderBarrow. The smoke from the flames was annoying, but not so bad that we couldn't breathe.

We approached another door and yet another guard opened it. I could see a stairway leading down. I caught my breath, feeling suddenly claustrophobic. Jason didn't look all that happy, either, but we kept our silence as we made our way down the stairs, swept along by the rest of the vampires. Again, I couldn't help but wonder—had I made a mistake?

When we got to the bottom of the stairs, the hall opened into a large chamber that looked like a nightclub that had jumped the shark. Only this nightclub was lit by lanterns rather than lights, and the music was from a live band. Here, I saw plenty of women, many of them with their fangs down. Kython had no dearth of female companionship. I glanced around, rather surprised that I wasn't seeing any collared women, though.

Kython dropped back to my side. "What do you think of my new digs?"

I glanced around at the elaborate red and black tapestries that cloaked the walls, the velveteen furnishings that looked worn and tattered, the gilt-edged photo frames, and the heavy wood tables, and thought this would be one of the most claustrophobic and depressing places to live. But I plastered on a smile.

"Well, it's more elaborate than your first quarters that I remember." I took a chance and added, "I see a lot of collared men, but..."

"But no collared women? There's good reason for that," he said. "I don't want my slaves and bloodwhores intermingling. No need for unplanned pregnancies here. Babies and vampires don't mix, and while I have no problem sinking my teeth into a ripe, gorgeous woman, I will abide no baby-killers under my roof." He sounded so serious that I wondered what had happened to make him adopt the practice.

"Well, for that, I and everybody else in my party would thank you." I happened to catch his eye, and we stared at one another. He dropped his guard for a moment and I saw beyond the cocky vampire. In its place, I caught sight of a war-weary Theosian and immediately, I recognized the feeling.

Before I could stop myself, I blurted out, "It's been a long road, hasn't it?"

He paused, then nodded, still serious. "Too dark and too long in some ways. I cannot help what I am, but I've changed in the past few years. I've seen the darker side of human nature in a way I never expected to, and decided that I will never willingly go beyond some boundaries that others—humans included—have no qualms breaking. Fury, every woman in this bunker has come voluntarily. I take slaves without guilt from the men, but women...if they are here it's because they have chosen to be here. And in case you had any doubt, you and your friends will be safe tonight." Abruptly, the mood shifted and he turned and sauntered up to his throne.

I let out a long breath, realizing that Kython and I had just experienced a relationship-defining moment. Our masks had dropped and we had seen each other for who we truly were.

I returned to the others. Thor had been watching me and now, he nodded with a faint smile.

"We'll be safe tonight," I said, fully believing it.

Kython sat on his tattered velvet throne and held up his hand. The music stopped.

"We have guests with us tonight. They are under my protection and you know what that means. A no fangs–on approach. Wayalin, please show Queen Fury and her friends to a guest room." He waved his hand again and the music started up.

A lovely female vampire, a gorgeous blonde with long, sleek hair, wearing a leather halter top and black jeans, approached us. "I'm Wayalin. Welcome to Kython's World. Follow me, please."

She sounded like a tourist guide, but I said nothing as we fell in behind her. We followed her to a suite of rooms with an adjoining bathroom. The bathroom had been modified to include a composting toilet and a working shower, though the hot water tank was powered by a wood fire.

"The water tank refills itself, the way we've rigged it up. I'll light a fire if any of you want showers."

"I don't know if that's necessary, though some hot water to wash our hands and faces would be helpful." I didn't want to wait for the time it would take to heat up as much water as a shower would require, and there were too many of us for the water tank to manage.

"I'll have a basin brought in with water for washing, and also some food. We have some bread and cheese if you'd like, and there's tomato soup." She sounded a little too bright, a little too eager.

I glanced closely at her and saw that her fangs had descended. She was too aware of us, I thought. Too thirsty.

"That's kind of you. Thank you." I took a subtle step away, and Thor, who was again watching, took a step forward. As he shifted position, she flinched and backed off, her fangs sliding out of sight.

"I'll have it brought right in." She turned and hightailed it out of the room.

"She's a thirsty girl," I said, watching her go.

"She is at that," Thor said. "But vampires have no power over the Elder Gods, and she knows well enough to leave us alone."

When we were alone, I thought about discussing our situation, but decided against it. The room could easily be bugged, and I didn't want Kython listening in, regardless of whether I considered him true to his word.

"What do you think of this place?" Jason asked.

"I think we're better off discussing other things," I said pointedly. "We don't know whether the walls have ears or not."

"Good point," he said, dropping onto one of the sofas.

There were four rooms—two bedrooms, a sitting

room, and a bath. They were furnished in the best velvet and leather money could have bought, but a tsunami and a decade had left them shabby and worn. I felt like we were in a tableau of a fading memory, and it occurred to me that while Under-Barrow and Willow Wood were thriving and felt vibrant and alive, here, everything felt worn and stifling.

There was a knock on the door, and when Elan opened the door, a servant brought in a handcart with a large metal basin filled with hot water, along with towels and soap. He lifted the tub onto the bathroom counter, and then silently left, trailing his cart behind him. He was a hefty man, but the collar he wore told me he was definitely in servitude to Kython.

I washed up first, along with Elan, and then Kendall and Shawna. After that, the men took turns. We were just finishing up when other servants arrived with dinner. I took a sniff of the soup to make sure it smelled like tomato—though I didn't think Kython would try to play a grisly practical joke on us. But it was definitely end of the season tomatoes, and I wondered where he got his produce. The bread was a little stale, but the cheese was fresh. We dug in, eating through the entire spread. Finally, our bellies were full. While I was still feeling chilled, we were protected from the rain and the zombies. We decided to turn in.

"I'm going to sit up for a while," Thor said.

I waited till the others went to bed—the women in one room, men in the other—before joining Thor in the main room. We sat in the dim light, not speaking.

After a few minutes, Thor waved his hand in the air and a mist descended around us in a whispering hush. Another moment, and he leaned back, looking more relaxed.

"Nobody can hear us now. I didn't want to do this earlier because with everyone awake, if they heard no noise, they'd be suspicious." He rested his hands on his belly and let out a wide yawn.

"Are you tired? I can keep watch for a bit."

"Tired? No, just a bit weary." He paused, then added, "Kython has changed, hasn't he? I noticed your demeanor toward him changed."

"I believe he has. He wasn't...*evil*...before, not exactly. But now, he seems to be taking his leadership seriously. I think the years since the shift have brought his Theosian nature to the surface again, though he tried to bury it." I tried to think of how to explain what I meant. "He's vampire, through and through, but Coyote isn't a malign god, even if he does dabble in chaos. I think the destruction of Seattle, and watching civilization fall away from those thin veneers it masks itself with, brought out a side of Kython that he would have expressed fully if he hadn't been turned. Do you know what I mean?"

Thor scratched his beard. "I believe so. Sometimes a jaded nature is assumed, and sometimes it's brought on by circumstances outside your control. He played games with authority before, the cynical, flamboyant vampire. Now, he knows how much is at stake and his leadership isn't for show."

"Something like that." I frowned. "Kython is

dangerous but he's reasonable. Karl Shefford—Gino? He's dangerous, and he's power-hungry. It occurs to me that we really would do well to blow up the land bridge that connects our side of the inlet with his. We don't want him gaining easy access. I have a feeling he may be a problem in the future, if he continues holding onto that little throne he's built for himself."

"I concur. I'll discuss this with the other gods when we return to Willow Wood." Thor pointed to the bedroom with the other women. "You should get some sleep. I'll keep watch. Don't worry. I'm a god. I don't need to sleep very often."

I pushed myself up from the table. "Thanks. Thank you for everything, Thor. You help us out more than we have any right to ask."

"No, you have the right to ask. I don't answer every request. I can't, and too often, the requests are petty and self-serving. But something like this, for the greater good of the community? I'll help if I can. Like it or not, the gods are intricately bound up in the lives of mortals—and those like yourself, who walk between the worlds."

That brought up another question. I had once asked Hecate—long ago—about it, but I knew every god's answer would be different.

"Thor, how do you feel about Theosians? We're not true gods or goddesses—we're minor gods on one level, but we weren't born among yourselves. Do you see us as mutants? As worthy? Why do you accept us into your service?"

"You're in a thoughtful mood tonight, aren't you?" He broke off a chunk of the remaining bread and bit into it.

"I suppose so." I wasn't sure why I wanted to know what he thought, but Thor was one of the gods I interacted most with and his opinion mattered to me.

"When we were called back to Earth after the first World Shift, Gaia gave us the responsibility to watch over your kind again. Not direct orders per se, but it had become clear that you didn't do very well watching over yourselves. When the first Theosians were born, she summoned us and told us that since you were born from the remnants of the World Shift, the gods had a responsibility to guide you. It's not your fault your DNA was changed. So we accepted your existence into the new order. Without us, the lot of you—or at least most Theosians—would be at war with one another. Trust me when I say this—you cannot be left to your own devices."

I nodded. "That's pretty much what Hecate said. It still doesn't answer how you feel about us, though."

He laughed. "I feel about you—and other Theosians—the way I do about most mortals. Some I am fond of, you included. Some I would rather see put out of the gene pool. Now run on and get some sleep. Tomorrow we face the city and while the ghouls won't be walking above ground, the zombies will still be a terror to fight, and the bog-dogs. You need to be in top shape."

With that, I said good night and returned to the bedroom, where I curled up in a big bed next to Elan. Next thing I knew, morning had broken and she was waking me up.

KYTHON WALKED US to the outskirts of his compound. He had offered me his arm and I had taken it, though it felt weird as hell. But he would see me out as a queen, and I would show his people that I was, indeed, one. It was still an hour till sunrise, but we wanted to get an early start.

We reached the gate. There, Thor's chariot waited.

"Be cautious once you exit here. Go directly south, and you will find the address you are seeking. There are ghouls still prowling—but they will dive for cover around sunrise. But the zombies will be out hunting, and they are ravenous and continuous. They neither sleep nor rest, but simply wander the streets until their bodies disintegrate and they can wander no more. By now, a number of them are merely bags of rotting flesh, and others are reduced to skeletons. When the bones weather away, or are broken asunder, they chatter about in the remains, so watch out for skittering hand bones and jaw bones with teeth that can still bite and gnash."

I grimaced. "Sounds delightful. I think this will be our last trip."

"Then mayhaps I shall have to make a journey to *your* village to see you again." He winked at me, and I had a sudden vision of Kython and his followers descending on UnderBarrow and Willow Wood.

"Notify us first so we can prepare our people. We have become a fierce community of our own and we guard against invaders, though we still welcome the weary and the worn, as long as they follow our rules." I straightened my shoulders. "We strive to be a safe haven."

"But only for those who follow your lead. Your Majesty," he said, and this time there was no hint of sarcasm or teasing in his voice. "You are just as harsh as I am. Just as harsh as the man you warned us about to the north. You would evict someone in an instant if they broke the laws. Correct? You would destroy someone who tried to destroy your people. Correct?"

I nodded, staring again into his eyes. The crimson was from the color of blood, from his transformation into the dark journey of the underworld. But behind the color, his soul was still Theosian, vampire or not.

"You know the answer to that," I whispered. "Thank you, Kython. I would like to consider you an ally, if it comes to that."

He inclined his head. "And I would consider you our ally, as well. We'll speak more on this at a later time. We *will* meet again, Queen Kaeleen the Fury. Trust me. And with all good luck, it will be a welcome meeting. Now go, for we must get back into the bunker. Our guards will shut the gate after you've left. Be safe. Be swift. Be alert."

He turned and marched back toward the bunker with his retinue in tow. The guards on the outer gate waited for us. While they were human, they wore no collars, but I expected they still belonged to Kython and Kython alone.

Thor ushered us into the chariot, and as the doors closed behind us, we began to move.

A SHORT TIME later, Thor opened the chariot doors again. "We're here. Come quickly. I don't like the feel of this area."

We scrambled out, surrounding the staircase down to the basement. Sure enough, the doors were closed by a heavy padlock, and a spray-painted symbol marked the spot. It was the same symbol that Elizabeth had drawn for us. The steps leading down were broken and looked dangerous, but at least it was only twelve steps to the bottom and there were still railings on the side that we could use to steady ourselves.

"Did Argent or Elizabeth tell us any more about the basement these things are in?"

"It was the basement of some building that caved in during the tsunami," Elan said, pointing toward the mass of rubble that lay strewn to the sides. "Possibly an urgent care clinic or medical warehouse. I'm not sure."

"Then that means we need to be careful, because there may be another entrance in the ruins. We can't know for sure." I turned toward Thor. "What are your marching orders? I'm taking my lead from you on this one."

"Let me think for a moment." Thor cast a cautious eye along the street.

We were on top of a steep hill in the northern part of the city, though by now, the ruins and rubble were so strewn about that I couldn't begin to place what district we were in, or what streets we were on. Here and there, the skeleton of a building still stood, but everything looked gray and precarious in the overcast morning, and it took only a few moments before we spotted a zombie wandering our way. It didn't seem to have noticed us, but if it kept coming in this direction, it would smell us before long. Or see us. I wasn't exactly clear on what caught the zombies' attention, but it had to be something.

"Over there," I whispered, nudging the god's elbow.

He glanced across the street. "Where there's one, there will be others. Get down there and start working on that padlock. I'll ward this fellow off if he tries to come at us."

Before I could head down the steps, Hans slipped in front of me, along with Zed. Elan and Jason were next, and Tyrell and Wheel brought up the rear. Kendall stayed up top with Thor, Fortune, and Shawna to fend off zombies.

Hans examined the lock. "Did they, by any chance, give you the key?"

I shook my head. "I can't believe I didn't think to ask."

"I asked," Elan said. "But in the scramble to get to Willow Wood, they dropped it. We'll have to either bust the lock open or pick it."

Wheel cleared his throat. "Let me take a stab at it. I learned to pick locks when I was younger."

We shifted positions. Wheel sorted through the gear in his belt-pack and pulled out a set of lock picks, quickly going to work on the padlock while behind us, Tyrell and Elan kept a watchful eye up the stairs. A moment later, I heard a faint *click* and the padlock opened up. I held my breath as Wheel slowly opened the door. The creak of the hinges sounded loudly in the morning air and the next moment, Kendall peeked down at us.

"Get a move on. The zombie heard that and he's coming this way. There are a couple more figures behind him and I have no doubt they're Meat-bag's pals." She jerked her thumb over her shoulder. "Thor says we'll prevent them from coming down the steps, but if you would hurry it up and find what you're looking for, he'd much appreciate it." She rolled her eyes, but then vanished back out of sight.

"Zombies. Come on. We need to get a move on." I motioned for Wheel and Zed to enter the base-ment. "Keep your eyes open and listen for anything that sounds like it shouldn't be here."

A cold breeze passed through me and I shiv-ered. It wasn't gusting much, even with the rain. I looked around, but couldn't see anything.

Queet, are you here?

I am, Fury. So are the ghosts. There are more spirits here than I've seen in a long while.

Did one just pass through me?

Yes, the poor soul looks lost. I think she senses

the fire within you—she's drawn to it. She's hungry for life, hungry for comfort. You need to be cautious, because she's following you and so are several others. I can try to run them off, if you like.

Please do.

I waited, wondering whether he was having any success. The hairs on my neck were standing up and I could feel the tension around me. But my attention was immediately diverted when Wheel yelped from just inside the door. He drew his sword and with one word, shook me out of my worry about ghosts.

"Zombies. They're in the basement. Your Majesty, get back now!"

Chapter 8

"I CAN'T, THEY'RE fighting zombies up top. We'll have to take care of these ourselves." I swung my scabbard around to my side, smoothly withdrawing Xan, the hilt pulsing in my hand as I wrapped my palm around it. I'd kept up practice, though I hadn't had much call to use her for a while. I sensed a faint quiver of excitement and realized that I was glad to be back in the thick of things for a change.

Zed looked at me, then nodded. "Yes, Your Majesty. Please be careful."

"I'm not stupid. I won't play the heroine unless I need to." I motioned for him to move in. "How many are we looking at?"

"I think there are at least five or six."

And then we were in the building and spreading out. It was dark, but Jason cast a Light Up spell and the room lit up enough to see what we were facing. There were stacks of supplies, shelf after shelf of them, but between us and the cache were several figures—all zombies from what I could tell. Though come to think of it, ghouls could be hanging out down here, given the darkness. But when the light had come on, I hadn't heard any shouts of pain so most likely we were just facing zombies.

I quit thinking then as Zed went in swinging, along with Hans. They took on one of the creatures as Greta and Tyrell tackled another. I nodded to Elan and we headed off another zombie while Jason and Wheel took on another. There were still three coming our way.

Elan and I took opposite sides, and I brought Xan around at shoulder level, aiming for the neck or what there was left of it. The zombie had half-rotted away and was looking pretty ripe. I wasn't sure what kept them together so long, but it had to be something in the virus. Whatever the case, the zombie had almost no guts left to digest anything, but was still ravenous. He—it had been a man—was gnashing his teeth, arms out in front, trying to reach us. The zombies moved fairly slowly compared to the living, but they never stopped, never tired, and eventually, they could run down just about any creature that needed to rest. They could also climb steps, though climbing trees was more difficult.

The side of my blade bit deep against its neck. I kept Xan razor sharp. She clipped into him and smoothly took off the head. It rolled on the ground toward Elan, eyes still moving, teeth still gnashing away. The body suddenly flailed, but didn't fall.

That was one of the problems with zombies. They kept going until they were a hundred tiny pieces. I brought Xan around for another swing at the torso, attempting to cleave it in two while Elan began slicing through the head. There was no splatter of blood—but the rancid juices from the slowly decaying corpse were dangerous for any open cut or way into the bloodstream. I dodged a spray, darting to the left when the torso came off the legs.

Elan split the pelvis of the zombie with a well-aimed blow and the legs toppled over, still attempting to move but unable to right themselves. The headless torso was attempting to drag itself along but Elan and I took turns carving it up, taking care to obliterate the hands so that they couldn't skitter along the floor.

Finally, we had destroyed the zombie.

We looked up to see that Zed and Hans, and Greta and Tyrell were on to their second opponents. Jason and Wheel had just finished taking down their zombie, and there was one left. Wheel motioned to Elan and they darted forward to engage it, while Jason and I regrouped.

"Holy crap," I said. "I forgot how tough these freaks are."

"Yeah, me too." Jason was looking pale. In fact, he looked about ready to faint.

"You all right?" I rested my hand on his arm. "I know this is tough on you."

"*Tough* doesn't begin to describe it, but I need to do this. I'm tired of feeling scattered and afraid. I'm tired of jumping at shadows." He glanced down at me—Jason was a tall man compared to me. "I never told you about what I encountered out on the realm of Chaos. But it was far worse than these zombies."

I stared at him for a moment. I had thought he couldn't remember what he saw out there, but now I wondered if he had just done his best to black out the memories because they were so bad. I glanced back at the others, who had managed to take down the rest of the zombies.

"Can you strengthen your Light Up spell so we can see what's in here easier?"

He nodded, holding out his hands. A moment later, he whispered a cantrip and the illumination in the room grew brighter, waves of light rolling off his fingers. Looking more settled, he let out a deep breath.

"Magic calms me down," he said, looking at me.

"Then it's good you've got the store." I glanced around. There didn't seem to be any more zombies, although given the shelves of goods scattered every which way, it wouldn't be hard to miss someone in the jumble. "Work in pairs of two. We want every medical supply that seems viable. Check expiration dates. Anything up to a year older than the date, we take."

Wheel dashed up top to check how Thor was doing, and to bring back the storage bags. He returned, a look of alarm on his face. "There are a lot of zombies up there, but Thor's managing to hold them off."

"I've got news for you—there are more zombies on the way here, too. I just scouted ahead in the basement. There's a broken door from what used to be the building upstairs. Looks like they can smell or hear us." Zed pointed toward the far end of the basement, which was out of range of the light spell. "You might want to move it."

I nodded. "Get busy, people. Don't bother looking at the dates, just fill these bags up." I grabbed a bag and headed toward the nearest shelf. It was filled with bandages and supplies. As I swept armfuls into the bag, I wondered if the trip had really been worth it. Most medicines expired after a certain time. But then again, a number of things—like the bandages and splints and even some of the packaged foods still here—had long shelf lives. I quit worrying and just began filling my bag.

As we worked our way through the shelves, handing bags to Wheel and Elan to run up to Thor, I suddenly heard something on the other side of the shelf that I was working on. I dropped my bag and quickly drew Xan, swinging around the other side. But it wasn't a zombie I was facing. Instead, scrambling for a hole in the wall was a little girl. At least I thought it was a girl. I dove, grabbing hold of her arm and yanking her back toward me. She was clutching a pocket knife and she swiped at me. I caught her arm before she could slice me and squeezed just hard enough to make her drop the knife. She whimpered but then crumpled, as if resigned to whatever fate I had in store for her.

I knelt, putting my sword on the floor next to me, and took hold of her shoulders. "What's your name?"

Her eyes widened and she shook her head, frantically trying to get away. Still, she made no sound.

The fear on her face told me more than I needed to know.

"Come on. There are zombies, but we're taking care of them. We won't let them get you."

She pulled at my grip, trying to break free, but I had a good hold on her. "Elan! Come here."

Elan popped around the corner, pausing as she saw the girl. "What did you find?"

"She was headed toward that hole in the wall. She's probably been living in there. Take a quick look, please."

As Elan knelt down to peek inside the hole, Jason appeared.

"We've got to hurry. More zombies are on the way both down here and topside. We've got twelve bags of supplies, along with a few boxes of unopened survival rations. I'm not…" His words drifted off as he took in the scene.

"Do you have any form of sleep spell? I want to sedate her so we can get her out of here without a problem," I said.

Elan popped back out of the hole. "Nest, all right. There's food and a few pictures that are pretty beat up. Looks like she's alone."

"We take her with us," I said.

Jason removed a small box from his pack. "I have some powder. It should work on someone her size."

The girl was still struggling, even though the look on her face told me she knew she was no match for us. But I didn't want to take a chance on having her break and run. For all she knew, we were slavers or hungry for human flesh or in league with the zombies. She didn't seem to be responding to what I said very quickly, and I wondered just how long she had been down here.

Jason blew the powder in her face and a moment later, she collapsed in my arms, breathing softly. He picked her up, then turned back toward the exit.

"We need to go," he said, striding toward the door.

Elan and I grabbed our bags and hurried after him. I could see Zed about to engage the nearest zombie. Behind that one, there were far too many heading our way.

I shoved my bag into Elan's hands and raced toward Zed and Wheel, sweeping up a bottle of booze that had rolled off one shelf near me and smashing the neck on the wall as I ran.

"Grab an empty sack!" I held up the booze, the liquid splashing a little on the ground.

Wheel picked up on my intention and grabbed a few more bottles of the alcohol, along with two of the spare sacks. He ripped them open and then broke the bottles, saturating the burlap. I dumped my booze on top.

"I'll spark it after you throw them!"

Wheel wrapped a rock in the sacks to give them weight, then heaved them in front of us as Zed jumped to the side. I conjured up just enough of a spark between my fingers to leap to the sack. The alcohol ignited, and the sacks burst into flames, spreading along the length of the cloth.

"Run, Your Majesty," Zed said, pushing me toward the door.

I dodged out of the way as Zed and Wheel smashed a crate of the booze onto the burning sack, breaking the bottles with the impact. A massive flame roiled up as they turned to follow me. The zombies couldn't get through the firebreak and we managed to scramble up top and slam the door behind us, locking it again with the padlock.

Thor had called down lightning from the clouds, and it struck near the zombies that were coming toward us on the streets.

"Into the chariot!" Thor jabbed his thumb toward the chariot and we scrambled in. When we were all there, Thor slammed the door and we were off, the goats racing like thoroughbreds.

I leaned back against the wall of the chariot, then looked over to where Jason was sitting with the little girl. She was asleep, draped next to him, curled up beneath a blanket.

"Who do you think she is?" he asked.

"Can she hear us?"

"No, that powder will knock her out for a while. Probably a good thing. I doubt she's slept much over the years."

I turned to Elan. "What did you see in her nest?"

Elan handed us a couple of faded photographs. "Just these. Looks like maybe her family?"

The pictures showed what looked like a family—a woman holding a baby, a man, and a teenaged boy. "Maybe her parents and brother?"

"Could be. She looks about eight or nine, so the tsunami had to have come through about the time this was taken, if that's her as a baby. She couldn't survive on her own at that point, so her family—or at least somebody—had to have made it for a while to take care of her."

"We'll only know if we can get her to communicate. There was nothing else in her nest?"

Elan shook her head. "No. Well, food wrappers and empty water bottles. She was obviously living off what was stored in the basement."

Weary, and feeling jarred because of the zombies, I lay down on one of the cushions and closed my eyes. Before long, I had drifted off.

WHEN I WOKE up, the chariot had stopped. Everybody was outside except for Elan, who was watching over me. I blinked and rubbed my eyes as I sat up.

"I had no intention of sleeping that hard. I've been extra tired lately and I don't know why. So, where are we?" I squinted, looking around.

"We're on the edge of Wild Wave Inlet, near the World Tree. There's a ferry coming from the Arbortariam to pick us up. Thor contacted Jerako. Meanwhile, we're keeping a low profile so we don't attract more zombies. It's about three p.m. Took that long for Thor to navigate through the city. It's a mess, he said. Torn to pieces. There's nothing left here, Fury." She hung her head. "Seattle truly is a city of ghosts."

I stretched, then cautiously stepped around the bags and scattered blankets to the door. We had descended an embankment to the edge of the water. The foliage along the side of the ravine was thick and lush. The others were keeping watch, and I saw Jason standing with the little girl in hand. She looked confused, shading her eyes from the light.

I walked over to them, and when she saw me, her eyes lit up—just a little bit, but enough that I knew she recognized me as safe.

"How is she?" I asked.

Jason glanced down at her. "She seems calmer. She hasn't let go of my hand since she woke up. She hasn't said a word, either."

I knelt, moving slowly so I didn't frighten her.

"Hi. I'm Fury. Do you have a name?"

She looked at me for a moment, biting her lip. I wasn't sure if she had understood me.

"Can you understand me? Do you know what I'm saying?"

She paused, staring into my eyes, then nodded.

I frowned. "Can you speak?"

Another moment, and then she shook her head. She pointed toward her throat, lifting her chin so that I could see a long pale mark across the flesh. I blinked. It looked like an old knife wound, and I nodded at Jason to take a look.

A moment later, Elan joined us. I turned to her.

"Can you take her back to the chariot and give her something to eat and drink? I want to talk to Jason alone for a moment." I nodded at the girl, and Elan caught my meaning.

"Of course, Your Majesty."

At that, the little girl jerked and looked at me,

blinking. Elan took her hand and led her back to the chariot. I turned back to Jason.

"Someone, at some time, cut that little girl's throat. It looks like a clean cut, not jagged, and it healed up, so either she's the luckiest kid on the planet, or someone else sewed her up before she could bleed out. I wonder if there's any way to ever find out the story. But it also may answer why she can't speak. Her vocal cords may have been severed during the attack."

"When she woke up and saw all of us sitting around, she scrambled close to me, but after a while, when nobody reached for her, she seemed to calm down. Elan also found a toy stash on one of the shelves, and she picked up a doll that still looked intact. The girl looked at it, then at Elan like she had no idea what to do with it."

"I have a feeling she hasn't been a little girl for a long time. She probably doesn't know what 'play' is." I sighed. "We'll have to have the healers work with her, see if they can help her." I glanced at the water. "How long till the Greenlings get here with that ferry?"

"Probably an hour or so."

I shaded my eyes to keep the drizzle out, then glanced back at the ravine. "How far to the World Tree?"

"Too far. Don't even think about it." He paused, then put his hand on my arm. "Kae, the world's all topsy-turvy but remember, we're family. You have to let some things go. You have to let them be. This city's done for. It was already done before the tsunami. The government was corrupt, people were dying. Their deaths were just slower than they are now. It's time to build new, on top of the ashes."

"I wonder..." I was feeling cold and shivery and bleak. "I wonder if we should bother rebuilding at all. Why? Just so someone can come along and bring it all down again? You'd think we would have learned the first time, but nope. Lyon and his bunch, and the government as well... So many would-be despots and dictators who ignored history and thought that this time, they would be able to control forces over which nobody has control."

Jason wrapped his arm around my shoulders. "I know, Kae. It's a harsh world and I'm pretty sure it will get a lot harsher before anything evens out. But there are good people in the world, and you and Tam are good leaders. You'll lead Willow Wood in the right direction."

"I hope so," I said. I paused as an energy I hadn't felt in a while crept into my mind. The next moment, my inner Trace screen lit up. An Abomination was nearby, tracking on a course right toward us. "Crap. Abom! Get everybody in the chariot."

Queet, are you there?

I am. I see it, Fury. It's a big one, in-body. It's taken over a zombie and it's coming this way on the run. Apparently, it can make the zombie's body move a lot faster.

Hell and high water. All right. We're taking it. Are you sure?

Yes, I'm sure. We have no choice. Scope it out while I tell the others.

As Queet whisked off to scout out the Abom, I turned to Thor and Zed, who were anxiously standing in front of me. Jason was busy ushering the others back to the chariot.

"There's an Abom coming in this direction. While I doubt it can hurt Thor, it can take out everybody else. And it won't leave. It can sense the life force here. It's taken on the body of a zombie, so it's not going to be easy to take down."

"You want my help?" Thor asked.

I hesitated. "That would be useful, but what about the others? We can't just leave them locked up in the chariot. I'm going to have to shift the creature over to the Crossroads in order to take it out. So draw me a good-sized cross in the dirt, please."

Zed shook his head. "I can't let you do this, Your Majesty. His Lord Tam would kill me if something happened to you."

"His Lordship Tam knows that my duties to Hecate include taking out Aboms and that when one is near, I have to go after it. This thing is coming our way. It will be here before the Greenlings arrive with the ferry. And it won't budge if it thinks a free meal is around." I slapped my thigh, bringing my whip to bear. "You can stay if you want, but don't get in the way. You can't take the zombie down in the usual way. I have to find the soul-hole to destroy the creature."

Fury, incoming! It's on the perimeter and coming over the edge of the embankment.

I whirled at Queet's warning, motioning for Zed to get back.

There it was, slipsliding its way down the ravine toward us. I assessed its movements as I watched.

It was moving faster than the zombies moved, by a good sight, and the light in its eyes was aware in a way that zombies' eyes weren't. There would be no good end to this unless I managed to dislodge the Abom from the body. Even then, I'd play hell because if I could hit the soul-hole and send the Abom packing, the zombie body would probably revert to its former status, and that in itself pro-vided a major danger. I needed to take it to the Crossroads where it couldn't attack anybody else, but I needed backup. Backup that Queet couldn't give me.

I quickly turned to Zed. "Listen, I need to take this out on the Crossroads. Somebody has to go with me because once I tackle the Abom, I won't be in any shape to take on the zombie."

"I'll go with you," Thor said.

I stared at the god. "But who's going to watch over everybody here?"

"Zed's a good man and Hans will stand in my stead. You have a top-notch team here, Fury. Use them to your advantage." Thor held my gaze and I realized that he saw through me. I didn't want to put anybody in danger. Coming back to Seattle had been my idea, and if anybody bit the dust, I'd be responsible.

"Everyone on this team volunteered, Your Maj-esty," Thor said, so softly I almost didn't catch his words. "You are not an executioner, regardless of how you feel at times."

I let out a long breath and turned to Zed. "Get Hans from the chariot. Watch over everybody until we get back. If the Greenlings arrive, don't wait too long before leaving. Trust me."

Zed winced, looking like he'd rather do anything else in the world except obey me, but he finally nodded. "Very well, Your Majesty."

I turned to Thor. "Can you get to the Crossroads yourself, or do you need a lift?"

"I can land there, Fury. Lead on and I will follow. I drew your cross over there." He pointed toward a long gash in the dirt where he'd marked out a cross. The arms were about five feet wide each, which gave me a good area in which to work.

I headed over to it, keeping my eye on the Abom. As Zed and Hans stationed themselves in front of the chariot, I held my whip in my right hand, and prepared myself for the jump. I'd been out on the Crossroads recently with Hecate—she kept me at it to make sure I didn't stumble when I needed to cross over. But it had been awhile since I had taken an Abom with me.

Queet, are you ready?

I'm ready. Does Thor know where to go?

I'm not sure, to be honest. I glanced over my shoulder. "Meet us at Hecate's cauldron on the Crossroads. Do you know where that is?"

Thor nodded. "I can find my way. I'll be there."

I turned back to the Abom, waiting until it saw me and sped up. I was candy to a baby. Aboms could sense me, even as I could sense them. I stood poised, waiting as he neared the cross. The moment he stepped into the circle surrounding the crossroad, I swept my hands up over my head and clasped them together, holding the whip between them. I focused on Hecate's cauldron as everything around me began to blur, and then we were out on the Crossroads.

THE CROSSROADS WAS a realm of perpetual mist and fog, a place where all worlds met and all paths crossed. The Elder Gods worked here, and some of them were endemic to this space. Hecate was bound to this realm, more so than in Olympus. Mercury and Hermes passed through on their errands. Janus, the god of two faces and gateways, skulked in the shadows, as well as Papa Legba, the master of Voudoun through whom all requests must come for those who followed his path. Time didn't exist here, and yet all times met and mingled in this place.

As I landed, my gaze first fell on Hecate's cauldron. At the center of a Y-juncture, the massive cauldron sat near a yew tree that sheltered a bench. A signboard sat near the cauldron, which read:

Stand at the Crossroads
State your claim
To seal the deal,
Strike the flame.

I had never kindled a fire in the cauldron, since I was already bound to the goddess. But others came to chance a request, and see what the Lady of the Night had in store for them.

I stood, my breath visible in the air. To all directions, on all sides of the roads, fallow fields stretched as far as I could see, littered with undergrowth and rocks and filled with dried grasses that sang in the wind, their susurration a mournful melody.

Shaking my head, I focused, and seconds later, the Abom appeared. The crossover would have shaken him up, though. That was one saving grace.

Queet?

I'm here.

Where's his soul-hole?

I'm looking.

I raised my whip, backing away. Another moment and Thor landed to my right, looking startled. I didn't have time to ask why, but kept my focus entirely on the Abomination, trying to circle around toward his back.

Soul-holes were usually found in the base of the neck, but I had a problem given the Abom was in a zombie vehicle—the soul-hole could close up and basically give him a bonus immunity to my attacks. I could just leave him on the Crossroads, but that wasn't an option in my mind. He'd wander until he found a way back to our realm. Or another realm. Either way, I didn't feel comfortable leaving a menace like him in-body.

Queet, I need you to divert his attention once you've found his soul-hole.

I don't think that's going to be a problem. Queet misted around behind the Abom and the creature turned. *His soul-hole is shining clear, but it's beginning to fade so you'd better hurry.*

The Abom turned, looking for a free and easy snack—spirits provided a lot of sustenance, and while Aboms didn't favor them over the living, if they were near and easy for the picking, an Abom wouldn't turn down a ghost. I shifted, darting behind it as the Abom focused on Queet. I brought my whip up, raising it over my head, and circled it with a loud series of cracks. The sound buoyed me up as a surge of adrenaline raced through my veins. I moved in, grateful that the zombie had been a short man, so it wasn't such a difficult target. Narrowing my focus, I forced all of my will into sending the Abom home, into disrupting his existence and splitting him asunder from the body he had taken over. The energy spun and soared, leaving me dizzy with both power and frenzy.

I brought the whip to bear and it crackled, flames soaring into the air, breaking the silence with snaps and sparks. The only thing I could see was the soul-hole now, every fiber of my being focused on disrupting the flow of energy that looped through the zombie's body. I let the fall of the whip fly, the sound piercing the air as it landed true, lancing the soul-hole.

The Abom shrieked, whirling around and lunging for me, and I stumbled back as a brilliant green light began to pulse from the base of its neck, from where I had split open the soul-hole. The Abom was bleeding out, his energy oozing out of the zombie's body as the force of my will and my attack sent him sailing home to Pandoriam whence he had first come. But as the Abom fled the body, the zombie kept coming.

My energy was quickly sliding off like a cloak falling to the ground. Attacking an Abom left me a shattered wreck—an occupational hazard of my duty for Hecate. But as I tried to dive out of its way, my mind was so scattered that I could barely see. I tripped, sprawling in front of the zombie that was lurching my way.

It was about to pounce on me when a shadow fell across my body and Thor stood there, Mjölnir in hand. With the hammer he landed a solid blow broadside of the zombie's head and the head went flying, leaving the neck to spout all sorts of vile ichor.

With one hand, Thor reached down and pulled me out of the way. With the other, he broadsided the zombie's torso, sending it sprawling toward the yew tree. I could barely comprehend what was going on, the effects of exiling the Abom had hit me so hard. I struggled to sit up.

Queet, are you there? It was all I could do to ask.

I'm here, Fury. Thor's smashing the zombie. Hold on. Can you get off the Crossroads without help?

I don't know. It's been so long since I've had to do this that— I stopped, unable to compose the end of the thought. I moaned and leaned to one side, vomiting into the straw-like grass. My stomach was empty, so all that came up was clear bile, but the dry heaves had hit me and I retched over and over until a trickle of blood ran down the side of my chin. I tried to wipe it away but all I could manage was to turn over and fall on my back.

Queet, I need help.

Thor's coming, Fury. Hold on.

The sky was beginning to waver in and out—or perhaps it was my consciousness wavering—but before I closed my eyes, I saw Thor's smiling face, staring down at me.

"Fury? Can you speak? Come on, I'll get you off the Crossroads."

The next moment, I felt him lift me up and, as every muscle in my body screamed against the movement, he started forward. It hurt so bad that I closed my eyes and tried to will myself to pass out. But that didn't happen until we began to make the jump off the Crossroads. As everything shifted, I couldn't hold it together any longer. I closed my eyes and gave into oblivion.

Chapter 9

"FURY? FURY, CAN you hear me?" The voice was one that I recognized as familiar, but that I couldn't put a name to. But it sparked feelings of safety and comfort in me, and I let myself float in the sensation. "Fury? You need to wake up now."

I slowly opened my eyes and found myself staring into the face of an old friend. His eyes were crimson, spinning as I watched, and then the crimson spun into orange into yellow into green, a kaleidoscope of beautiful colors.

"Jerako?"

"Yes, it's me, Bonny Queen." The man behind the eyes was ten feet tall, created entirely of woven foliage. His arms and legs were branches, thickly padded with moss. His face was formed from woven leaves and twigs, and he was like a living statue, emerging from the very essence of Gaia. His aura sparkled and crackled, the magic of his life force sourced directly from the heart of the world. He was ancient, Jerako was, as old as the hills and older. The original green man, Jack in the Green, the *spirit of the wild*, all of these things he was, and yet—so much more.

"Where am I?" I tried to sit up, but my head was spinning. Every time I made the jump to the Crossroads to take care of an Abomination, I was left with a massive energy hangover and a migraine from hell.

I looked around, grateful that the light was low. I was in a small chamber, settled on a pile of cushions and pillows. Fairy lights sparkled through the air, illuminating the room. Jason and Elan were with me, and Thor, and I spotted Zhan in the corner. Zhan was a hedgemite, and he reminded me of a satyr, only instead of horns on his head, he had branches, and he was slight of build and lithe. He gave me a wave and I forced a smile through the pounding pain in my head.

"You're at the Arbortariam. You're safe for the night. Drink this." Jerako nodded to a cup full of steaming liquid that Elan was holding. "It will ease your headache and give you strength."

I eagerly accepted the cup. Most of what the Greenlings had to offer tasted like dried fungus and dirt, but it worked miracles. I had been on the receiving end of their care before. I gulped down the earthy tea, closing my eyes as it flooded my system with warmth and strength. The pain in my head began to subside, and I finished the cup and leaned back on the pillows.

"Where are the others?"

"They're safe, and eating dinner. The hedgemites are attending to them."

The Greenlings—basically Gaia's henchmen—had saved the hedgemite race from extinction, and now the hedgemites attended them, forever grateful for the favor.

After a moment, I felt strong enough to sit up. My body ached, my muscles were sore and tight. Even though I hadn't been in a direct fight with the Abom, the massive surge of energy that had flowed through my body when I sent him home to Pandoriam had basically pummeled me. I stretched slowly, wincing as my back popped.

Thor seemed to have heard that. "Good pop or bad one?" he asked.

"Good…I hope."

"One of the hedgemites will give you a back rub," Jerako said.

It sounded wonderful. "Thank you, I could use it. So, have the others filled you in on what happened?"

Jerako frowned. "If you mean with the Abomination, yes. And the city of ghosts. You should not go there again, Fury. It becomes more dangerous with each passing day, and I don't know how long it will be before simply entering the city becomes a death warrant."

"I tend to agree," I said. "Before long, all that will be left there will be the dead—both the walking dead and those in the spirit world. Although I have to say, I'm grateful that we managed to rescue the little girl. I wonder how many like her are left there, hiding in the shadows, doing what they can to scrounge out a living while avoiding the ghoul packs and the zombie hordes. I suppose there's no way to rescue everybody who's still hiding there."

"There will always be those we can't save," Thor said. "We rejoice in the ones we can, and pray for the ones we can't."

"Jerako, I want to talk to you about something," I said, grateful for the tea. My thoughts were starting to clear.

"I'm actually thankful that you showed up here," Jerako said. "It saves us a trip to your village. We *do* have much to talk about. There is a growing danger that the trees are whispering about. One that will affect your entire world."

I really didn't want to hear that. The world had already been shaken up so much that it felt like we were still in a water globe, constantly being set into motion.

"If I could get some food, we can discuss matters." I struggled to get up, and Elan helped me. As they guided me over to a long table in the corner, I saw that it was piled high with fruit and cheese and bread. Zhan brought me a cup of hot broth that tasted infinitely better than the tea had. As I ate, I began to tell Jerako about the village of the Frostlings.

JERAKO SAID NOTHING for a long time after I finished telling him what we had found. By now, I was used to the thoughtful nature of the Greenlings. They acted immediately when ordered by Gaia, but on all other things they took their time. Jerako had lived for tens of thousands of years, and that was a great many memories to sort through.

"We know there has been trouble throughout the woodland. The sentinels have sent reports about lycanthropes gathering under a banner. They are organizing, but we're not yet sure why. There was a report of something coming off the World Tree, something massive and dangerous. That was about a month ago, but then it seemed to disappear and we heard no new reports."

"An Abomination?" I asked, wondering why we hadn't been informed of it.

"No, not an Abomination. And it wasn't Lyon or any of the Elder Gods of Chaos either. The portal to that realm remains sealed shut, so firmly that I doubt that it will ever open again. But this was from somewhere high in the tree. The door flared to life with a brilliant blue light, and then faded. My sentinels sent word that whatever it was destroyed the zombies in the pit around the tree with the wave of one hand. A strange, cloaked figure, bathed in a nimbus of pale blue light, flanked by—"

"Four massive wolves," I said.

"How did you know?" Jerako turned to look at me.

"I had a dream that I was out on the Tremble and Rasheya was calling for me. She wanted to tell me something. I was trying to find her when a man passed by, and I was absolutely petrified when I saw him. He was cloaked in a wraith of blue fire, flanked by four giant wolves. I was terrified he would see me when he passed by, but he looked neither right nor left, simply marched on toward the edge of the Tremble. I had hoped to stop there and seek her out—Rasheya, that is. But there's no way we could have taken that route."

Jerako nodded. "The Tremble has become even more unstable and will soon be uninhabitable. I fear the Mudarani will have to move eventually."

"Why? They're bred for the energy—it's what makes them, *them*. And they live underground, where it doesn't penetrate." Jason looked confused.

Zhan fielded that one. "Because the energy of the Tremble now penetrates even into the soil itself, and below. Before long that will reach their underground caverns, and while they are definitely born and bred to handle the energy better than outsiders, they will not be able to stave off the effects of long-term permanent exposure."

I stared at the table, thinking about the incredible society they had built up. The Mudarani were a product of the Tremble as much as I was a product of the Sandspit. To think of them losing their home weighed heavily on my heart, and I thought perhaps we should reach out and offer them a chance to come live with us at UnderBarrow. I'd have to talk to Tam, of course.

"Why has the Tremble become so unstable?" Elan asked.

Jerako let out a soft rumble. It sounded a lot like a cat purring, only so much louder.

"The second World Shift was brought about not only by Gaia's wrath, but by the artifacts from the Weather Wars. Those ancient weapons were designed to destabilize weather patterns, and to interfere with the natural forces of the world. While the Tremble wasn't originally considered a natural force, it became inherently woven into the very essence of the planet.

"So when the Thunderstrike and the Earth Shaker were used, they set into motion a series of destabilizations that are still going on. Think of it this way: the use of those artifacts have mutated the planet. Gaia can't stop everything that's happening, and so right now chaos is running rampant, especially around the magical places like the Tremble and the World Trees. This is happening all over the planet. There is no telling how far reaching this will be."

I stared at the others, unsure of what to say. None of us had suspected that the world was still reeling and changing from what had gone down. I thought that perhaps Gaia had gone a little far with the last World Shift, but it wasn't for me to question. Now, I realized that the changes weren't over yet, and there was no telling what life would be like in another twenty years.

"What can we do about the Frostlings? Do you know what happened to them?" I decided the best question was the easiest one.

Jerako motioned to Zhan, and the hedgemite darted out of the room.

"That is something we can help you with. We got notification this morning about the village. They have been frozen in stasis, and that is something that I *can* abate. I will give you a scroll which, when read in the Frostlings' village, will break the paralysis and bring them back to life. They are in essence being held by the force found in Limbo. Someone siphoned energy off the realm of Limbo and used it in a spell against them. Whoever did this has to be an extremely powerful sorcerer, that much I can tell you. Either that, or he has power over the elements of winter and ice."

I caught my breath. "If the latter is true, then is UnderBarrow in danger? We are the Fae Court of Winter."

"If whoever did this does indeed have power over the frost and snow, UnderBarrow might well be a target. The Frostlings might be able to tell you who cast the spell on their village. I would ask that once you rouse them, you ask them to send word to us through the sentinels. Gaia will want to know."

As Zhan returned with a long ivory-colored tube, a sense of dread swept over me. We had thought we were starting to get things under control, that we were making headway on rebuilding our corner of civilization. Now, to learn everything was still shifting and changing? It all seemed too much.

"Of course," was all I said. I took the scroll. "How do we use this?"

"When you reach the borders of their village, remove the scroll from the tube. Then stand just inside the borders and read the words. At first they will look like a bunch of strange glyphs, but as you hold the scroll, the words that you need to know will appear. Don't worry about forcing any energy into it or trying to direct the energy. This scroll should break the curse, whatever the cause." Jerako paused, then added, "I don't want to rush you, but you should go. We need to find out what's going on, and I have a feeling the Frostlings can tell us. The sooner we can get this information to Gaia, the better."

I was still tired, but the headache had backed off and I could rest in the chariot on our way to Wyfair. Jerako's sense of urgency seemed to seep into me, and I felt the urge to depart.

"I think you're right. I can sense it. There's something going on that we need to know about, and its roots are deeper than any of us realize." I had no clue why I added the latter, but it rung true.

Jerako stood, towering over us. I looked up into those wisdom-filled eyes, holding his gaze, trying to absorb as much strength from his wisdom that I could.

When I looked at him, *truly* looked at him, the cares of the world seemed to drift away, swept into the stream of time that flowed behind him. He had seen so many wars come and go, lived through change after change after change as the world evolved. When I thought of the time that he had been on this planet, I understood how he could sit back and observe, how he could take his time even when things seemed urgent. In a way, Jerako represented the peace of mind and heart that I had always longed for, and for a moment I wished I could stay here in the Arbortariam with him, live my life in a quiet contemplation.

He seemed to understand what I was thinking, because he reached across the table, placing one of his leaf-covered hands on my shoulder. His touch was alive and vibrant, and I felt his energy blend with mine.

"The world marches on, even for the Greenlings, Queen Fury. Everything moves and advances. Everything evolves, whether it be from forced circumstance or natural progression. There is no use fighting it, we just learn to adapt and move with it. If the world were to remain in stasis, everything would stagnate and life would wither and die. Great upheavals bring great leaps in the metamorphosis of this world.

"Fear not, and weep not for the changes. While they may seem catastrophic to mortals, in the great scheme of things, they are mere blips on the timeline. Life will survive, and you should know more than most that the spirit resides long after the body is faded away. So be of good cheer, and face the future with a bright heart."

As he pulled away, I realized I was breathing easier. The Greenlings' magic was strong, and their words were even more powerful. I smiled up at him, my shoulders relaxing.

"Thank you, Jerako. I hope I can always count on you as a friend and ally. As soon as we have wakened the Frostlings from their paralysis, we'll ask them to send word to you. We'll meet whatever this new force is together."

Zhan led us into another chamber where the rest of our party waited. The little girl was clinging to Shawna, but when she saw us, she ran up to Elan and wrapped her arms around Elan's leg, clutching her tightly. Elan looked over at me.

"She's really taken to you," I said. "We can't go on calling her 'she' or 'the child.' We need a name for her."

Elan knelt by the girl and held her by her shoulders. "Do you have a name?"

The girl paused, looking confused. After a moment she nodded.

"If you can't tell us what your name is, until we can find out, do you mind if I call you 'Hope'?" Elan looked up at me and I nodded. It seemed a fitting name.

The little girl wrapped her arms around Elan's neck and hugged her tight. Elan stood up, lifting her in her arms. As we headed toward Thor's chariot, it occurred to me that we had gone into Seattle with one hope, and come out with another.

And you could never have too much hope.

WE TOOK ADVANTAGE of the ferry from the Arbortariam over to the Wild Wood to sleep. When we woke, I realized that I wasn't sure how many days had passed since we first left Willow Wood.

"We're nearing Wyfair. I let you sleep through the night. It's nearly morning." Thor motioned us out of the chariot. He had started a fire, and I put on a pot of porridge to cook. The rain was sleeting down so hard that it almost felt like hail. The ground was muddy and wet, and I realized we had hit the thick of autumn. I pulled my cloak tightly around me, huddling under one of the trees for shelter. Elan, Shawna, Kendall, and I took Hope with us into a nearby patch of bushes to relieve ourselves. Given the situation with lycanthropes there was no way anybody was heading out on their own.

When we returned to the fire, I saw that Thor had heated up a pot of water along with the porridge and had also made a large pot of tea. Elan scooped a bowl of water out of the cauldron for us to wash our hands in. Shawna and Wheel handed out bowls of porridge, and we huddled under the trees, trying to keep as dry as we could while we ate.

"How far are we from the village?" I asked.

"About half an hour's ride. I stopped here because I smell lycanthropes up ahead, and I wanted you awake and prepared in case we meet them. I'm hoping they haven't been in the village, tearing things up."

"Whoever is marshaling them must have a tremendous amount of power in order to take control of them. Lycanthropes don't bow to anyone except themselves. And even then, it usually takes fang to the jugular in order to produce submission." The thought of anyone strong enough to marshal all the lycanthropes under a banner was frightening. Over the past eight years they had grown in number, with fewer to thwart them.

We finished eating in silence. The knowledge that a group of lycanthropes was near was sobering, and nobody felt like talking much. There wasn't really much to say, and the less noise we made, the better. Finally, we climbed back in the chariot, and set out again. I held the scroll tube tight my hand, praying that it would be as easy as Jerako had said.

AT THE BORDERS of Wyfair, Thor told us to stay by the chariot while he checked out the village. I was nervous, wondering if the lycanthropes were near, but by the time he got back, we had seen neither hide nor hair of them.

"Everything looks much as we left it," Thor said. "Are you ready, Your Majesty?"

I nodded, stepping over the border into the village. "Here goes nothing."

I opened the scroll tube and shook the scroll out of it. Elan took the tube from me as I unrolled the parchment. It truly did look like a series of unintelligible glyphs, but as I stared at it, words begin to form out of the runes. I waited until the scroll had entirely translated, and then, taking a deep breath, I hold the scroll up and began to read.

What was bound, let be unbound.
What it was frozen, let be set free.
From sky to ground, from ground to sky,
Magic leap and magic fly.
That which slumbers, waken now.

What was stunted, let now grow.
By power of Oak and Holly tree,
that which I will, so mote it be.

There was a rumble under my feet as the earth began to quake.

Startled, I dropped the scroll and wavered as Zed reached out to steady me. As I clung to his arm, a wash of magic rolled through the village, rolling like a wave coming in from the sea. It crested around the houses and the frozen Frostlings, rising up to spiral around everything within the borders of Wyfair. It was as though a giant hush had been broken, and the village yawned and stretched its arms, wakening to life. I caught my breath, swept up in the swirl of magic, rising high on its currents. The power of the Greenlings swept around me, refreshing everyone and everything in its wake.

In that fraction of a second, everything shifted and the Frostlings awoke. Some tripped, falling to the ground, they had been so intent on an action when they were frozen. Others looked around, and the feeling of confusion raced through the streets, though no emotion showed on their frozen faces.

It was then that one of the Frostlings turned toward me. I recognized him.

It was the Guardian, the watcher over the village. He strode forward, and if I had not known what the Frostlings were like, I would have been terrified of the great creature that came toward me.

"Gracious Queen of UnderBarrow, Queen

Kaeleen the Fury, what are you doing in our borders? What happened to the wandering one? Where did he go?"

The Frostlings never sounded angry, but I thought I detected the nuance in his question.

"We were passing through and found your village frozen. We had to leave, but when we returned we stopped at the Greenlings and they gave us a scroll to free you from whatever spell was put on your village. Do you know what happened? Do you know who it was who attacked you?"

The Guardian nodded, glancing at the rest of the party. "Come, you must get under shelter. It is dangerous to travel on the roads when dusk is falling."

Thor brought the chariot up behind us as we followed the Guardian into the village proper. He led us to one of the log cabins that were scattered among the ice crystal buildings. Opening the door, he guided us into a large chambered room, bidding us to wait for his return.

As he left the building, shutting the door carefully behind us, I dropped into one of the chairs, enjoying the warmth of the cabin. While there was no visible source for heat, it was warm and cozy. Just as I had remembered, there was a small but functional bathroom off to one side. I peeled off my wet cloak, spreading it over the back of a chair, wishing for a towel to dry my hair with.

"How long do you think he'll be?" Zed asked.

"I don't know, but I'm grateful to be out of the rain, I'll tell you that. And I'm grateful that the scroll worked." I looked over at Hope, who was staring out of the window with wonder in her eyes. It suddenly occurred to me that she had probably never seen the forest, never seen trees like this. Present-day Seattle was a mishmash of rubble and vegetation that was quickly covering the old structures, but there were no tall trees left there. Once there had been, but the tsunami had taken care of that, sweeping them away like so many toothpicks.

"We're not far from home, at least," Jason said. "Given all the talk of lycanthropes, I'm hoping that Willow Wood hasn't been attacked in our absence."

"I've been thinking about that too," Elan said, her hands pressed on his shoulders.

I realized they were thinking about their daughter, worried about her safety.

"Aila is safe enough. UnderBarrow is highly protected, and as long as she's inside, she'll be all right. You know that Tam and Damh Varias keep a sharp eye on everything that's going on in the village." I didn't want them to worry. They risked so much in our service, and I wanted them to feel secure.

Elan was about to reply when the door opened, and the Guardian entered again. He was followed by two other Frostlings I didn't recognize.

"You will understand if I don't stand on ceremony," the Guardian said.

I nodded. "There are strange things afoot in the woods. We don't have time for small talk."

"You understand, then. The Alezakai Neshera and our Soothsayer have given me leave to speak for them. They are busy attending to business, and you will soon find out why." He took a seat at the head of the table, and we all gathered around.

"Please, tell us what you have to say. But first, I want to make sure you know that the lycanthropes are gathering. We don't know who's in charge of it, but there have been several attacks—vicious, brutal ones. And we know they are behind them." I leaned forward.

The Guardian stared at me for a moment before answering. "Yes, we do know this. And we know whose banner they gather behind. A man came off the World Tree. He comes from distant lands, although you will recognize the world of which we speak." He turned to look at Thor.

Thor frowned, his brows crinkling. "It cannot be a friend of mine. None of the gods would do this to you—at least none of those in Gudarheim."

"Oh," Guardian said, "I do not believe it is a *friend* of yours. And this is why you must know and take this knowledge back to your village and the gods who reside near there. The man who cast the spell on our village is well known in our history. First, to understand, you must know a little more about the Frostlings."

I was feeling impatient, wanting him to get on with it, but I said nothing. As with the Greenlings, the Frostlings worked at their own pace, and nothing you could do would shift that.

The Guardian sat back in his chair. "The Frostlings come from a mixture of races. Long ago, the Queen of the Winter Fae fell in love with an Ice Elemental. Somehow, a child was born of the union, and then another. It was thus that the race of Frostlings was born. Those children were cast out by both the Fae and Elemental worlds, who feared what the result of such a union might be. They were cast into Niflheim to live or die as they would. There, they clung together, and managed to survive. A frost giant found them, and took pity on them, and gave them powers from his own soul. The Frostlings prospered, and began to have children of their own. As their numbers grew, some began to leave Niflheim, crossing through the World Tree to this world. We are those who came into this world so many years ago. But when we were in Niflheim, we grew familiar with the entities who lived there. And some of them hated the Frostlings as much as they hated those who lived in Midgard, and as much as those who were mortal."

Thor let out a long breath. "It cannot be Loki. I know that he hasn't returned to this world yet. When the Elder Gods left, many of us chose to stay but he turned tail and ran. And from what Odin told me, he hasn't been back."

"Oh, it's not Loki," the Guardian said. "It's his child. Fenrir has crossed over to this world, and it is his intention to bring Ragnarök to bear."

Silence echoed through the room following his pronouncement. After a moment, Thor pushed himself to his feet and crossed to the window, staring out as he crossed his arms.

"Of course. That's why I recognize the energy. I have dealt with the Fenris Wolf before, but not for thousands of years." He turned, his face bleak. "If Fenrir is here, then he is probably looking to wake

Jörmungandr, his brother, the serpent at the heart of the world. Jörmungandr is the only one strong enough to fight against Gaia, even in her own body."

I didn't know a lot about the Norse pantheon, but what I knew was enough. "The man I dreamed of that crossed the Tremble? He had four great wolves with him. Could that be Fenrir?"

"I have no doubt of it," Thor said. "Fenrir can assume the form of a charismatic human, even more charismatic than his father. But he is fierce and wild, and where my brother understands the need for some diplomacy, Fenrir is feral and lives by tooth and fang. He is a danger to all who cross him. If he is looking to begin Ragnarök, then little can stop him. The lycanthropes would rush to his side, as they would understand his nature. And they will follow him as a leader."

"What can we do?" Kendall asked, her face bleak. She turned to Thor. "Can you enlist the other gods to stop him?"

Thor looked as though he'd seen a ghost. "We will try. I cannot promise, because my kind are fated to go under during Ragnarök. If this is truly the beginning of the great war, the scope of death will be unimaginable."

I wanted to cry. I wanted to go to sleep and wake up and have everything as it was even twenty minutes ago. There's always that moment when you find out something horrendous, when you learn of a tragedy beyond the scope of your ability to fix, where you long to reset everything, to step back in time to before you received the bad news. I didn't know what to say. Here I was, queen of the kingdom, and I was without words to comfort. There was no comfort as far as I could tell.

"Tell me this," Jason asked. "During Ragnarök, it's foretold that the gods fall. But does that mean all of the gods? Will Hecate and Zeus and the Dagda and Athena and Aphrodite and Ukko and every other god from every other culture die as well?"

Thor shrugged. "I don't know. I have no answers for you. But we need to get back. I have to talk to the others so we can plan how to proceed. For even during the World Shifts, the gods have never faced the end of days."

As we sat there in the growing dusk, all I could think about was everything that we had worked for, and how far we had come. Was it all in vain? Would Gaia be able to help us? Or had she somehow, in a desire to start over, set this in motion herself?

Chapter 10

WE ARRIVED HOME to find Willow Wood in an uproar. As we pulled into the village, Thor stopped and opened the door.

"I think you're going to want to see this, Your Majesty." He ushered me out of the chariot.

I looked around, startled to see so many guards on the outskirts flanking the road. They were armed and standing at attention, and I saw that Leonard was leading the unit. I walked over to him, and the entire unit dropped to one knee in formation.

"Stand. Now, tell me, what's going on?" I asked, casting a wary eye at the road beyond them.

Leonard and the other guards stood. He held my gaze, a stark look on his face.

"Your Majesty, welcome home. His Lordship has ordered us to guard all roads in and out of Willow Wood. There have been a number of attacks from the lycanthropes in the past two days. His Lordship has put a curfew on the entire village as well as UnderBarrow. No one is allowed in or out without permission, and everyone leaving the village must be accompanied by at least four guards. The only exception is for the hunters, and they are to hunt in large groups."

"It's lucky we gathered the harvests when we did," I said. Keeping a watch over the fields would have been a logistical nightmare.

"We have news about the lycanthropes," I continued. "Serious news. I want you present when we talk to the Sea-Council." I paused, not wanting to say too much because I didn't want the rumor mill starting. But then I leaned forward, up on my tiptoes, to whisper in Len's ear. "Our entire way of life is about to change again."

As I stood back, he caught my gaze, a bleak look in his eyes. Len had known so many changes in his life. He had only been fifteen when the second World Shift hit, and while he had hit a rough spot at that point, he had grown out of it into an impressive young man.

"Understood, Your Majesty."

"Find someone to take your place and jump in the chariot with us. We're going into the meeting as soon as we reach UnderBarrow. It's that serious." I turned, crossing back to the chariot. A few minutes later, Len joined us. He didn't ask what was wrong, for which I was grateful. I didn't want to have to go into the whole story a dozen times over.

We headed directly for UnderBarrow, skirting

the edge of the village. The moment we arrived, I sent Zed to summon the other members of the Sea-Council, and I sent Elan to ask Hecate to join us.

"Impress on her just how much of an emergency this is."

The rest of us, Hope in tow, headed directly for the Blue room. Wheel had gone ahead to find Tam, but before he was out of sight, Tam came racing down the corridor. Damh Varias was right behind him. Ignoring protocol, Tam grabbed me in his arms, spinning me around for a kiss.

"I'm so glad you're back and safe. I was so worried about you." He gave me another kiss, and I rested my head on his shoulder for a moment, grateful to be back in his arms. Then I stood back, including Damh Varias in my gaze.

"I missed you too, and thought about you every minute. But we have a situation that we must discuss now. Into the Blue room, because we cannot chance word of this getting out before we decide how to proceed."

Tam shot a quick glance over at Damh Varias, but the two followed me without question. By the time we got to the Blue room, Sarinka and Laren were waiting. A serving maid brought in large pitchers of mulled cider, along with a tray of sandwiches and cookies. Grateful for the fresh food, I motioned for her to leave as I filled my plate. There was no time to stand on ceremony, given everything we had learned from Jerako.

Tam crossed to my side, sliding his arm around my waist.

"My wife, what on earth could have happened to cause this urgency? Is it about the lycanthrope attacks?"

"Those are just the tip of the iceberg, and I use the word *iceberg* deliberately." I shook my head. "What we have to tell you is going to change the entire future for this village. We have a number of decisions to make, and we have to make them quickly." I carried my plate back to the table and took my place beside Tam.

A moment later, Hecate entered the room, with Elan behind her. The goddess looked over at Thor. "Is what Elan says true?"

"Yes," Thor said, and that one word was enough. Hecate took a seat beside him.

When we were all settled, I laid out what the Guardian of the Frostlings had told us. I figured it was best to start out with that news, because what had transpired in Seattle was of absolutely no consequence at this point. Soon, nothing about the city of ghosts would matter.

"*Ragnarök*," Damh Varias said, sliding back in his chair. "We all knew that someday it would come, or at least we had the warnings. But with each World Shift, it seemed less likely to happen." He straightened. "Your Majesty," he said, turning to Tam. "We must withdraw our soldiers from Verdanya. I know we only just sent them, but given this news, Willow Wood cannot be left without a full military contingent."

"Verdanya? What's going on in Verdanya?" I asked.

"While you were away—in fact, the very afternoon that you left—we received a plea for help from Verdanya. They were being overrun by lycanthropes. While Verdanya and Willow Wood have no love lost between us, I couldn't just turn away from their cry of help. So I sent a third of our troops down there to help out. It seems I was premature in my decision." Tam's expression was both terrible and fearsome. He was a foreboding man when he fell into his moods.

"We must pull them back. Fenrir could move at any time, and we have no idea of what he's planning." I turned to Thor. "Do you have any idea of the way this is going to play out?"

Thor leaned his elbows on the table, crossing his arms as he stared at Tam and me.

"It's hard to say. I know what the prophecies say, but they're not always literal." He turned to Hecate. "I'm sure you know all too well about how that works."

She nodded. "Yes, I found the same myself. But there is much truth within the prophecies, so it behooves us to examine them anyway. At least it may give us some clue of what Fenrir is planning."

"The last set of prophecies that we received from the Norns goes thus: At some point, Fenrir will begin the march and he will wake Jörmungandr. Next, the ice giants gather behind him for the second wave. Loki and the fire giants will herald the third wave. And then the world will split from the merging of fire and ice, breaking between the two."

I swallowed my bite of sandwich in a hard gulp. "What then?"

"Out of that hellhole, a new age will emerge. So

if we're to follow the prophecies, the next step is for Fenrir to waken Jörmungandr. Jörmungandr is the only one who can attack Gaia on a personal level, though he dare not kill her. If he kills her, he kills himself. But the world serpent isn't necessarily sane, and his movements cause great upheavals up on the surface of the planet. Perhaps not as great as the World Shifts that Gaia has rained down, but he can do a great deal of damage."

"Are we talking earthquakes? Volcanic eruptions?" I appreciated having some sort of guideline, but it occurred to me that it would be very helpful if the prophets of old would somehow manage to speak clearly rather than in riddles.

"Earthquakes, volcanoes, massive flooding. When you get down to it, Jörmungandr might as well be his own Weather Wars artifact. I'm pretty sure Gaia is aware of what's going on, and I have no doubt she's preparing for battle." Thor shrugged. "But even if she quells Jörmungandr, it won't do much good. Once Ragnarök begins, there's no stopping it."

"Can she kill Jörmungandr before this happens?" I wasn't at all sure about god-on-god action when it came to destroying each other.

"Perhaps, but it won't come without massive disruption. When Gaia goes to battle, you've seen what happens to the surface of the world." Thor stopped, and the room fell silent.

Damh Varias was the next to speak. "I think what we need to do is clear. I know you aren't going to want to hear what I have to say, but we have to close up UnderBarrow and retreat between the worlds. You have a duty to your people to protect them."

"Is that possible?" I asked. "Don't we have to *land* somewhere?"

Tam's eyes flickered but he turned to me. "No, we can stay between the worlds enclosed within our own little realm. We can also take UnderBarrow into the Shining Courts, where my parents exist and rule."

"But what of Willow Wood? What happens to the village?" Jason asked.

"Those choosing to come with us would be welcome. But if UnderBarrow moves, Willow Wood will be on its own. We could manage to fit the entire population into UnderBarrow for the move. Then we would have to begin anew wherever we set down." He thought for a moment, then turned to Damh Varias. "What of going back to Eire?"

Hecate broke in. "That will do you no good. No matter where you go on this planet, Ragnarök will touch the shores. If Jörmungandr moves against Gaia, the entire world is in danger."

"Shouldn't we warn people?" Sarinka asked, leaning forward. "Given a god is involved, you can bet the lycanthropes are gathering all over the world to follow Fenrir."

"And *how* would you have us warn them?" Hecate asked. "World communications are destroyed. It takes days just to reach the next village. Cell phones are gone, satellites still fly the skies but there's nothing down here for them to reach because we have no electricity to run all of the gadgets and technology that existed before. We have techno-mages, but they're busy trying to create lifesaving equipment to replace that which we've lost."

Sarinka shrank back. "Can we send messengers?"

"Oh, send out runners if you like, but it's a suicide mission and will take far longer than Fenrir is likely to give us. But you are correct in the assumption that the lycanthropes are likely gathering around the world. Fenrir is a god; he can move as he chooses throughout the world. In the blink of an eye, he can be on another continent. And before you ask, yes, the gods *could* go world hopping, but how many people do you think are going to listen to us? All they're going to do is beg us to save them and we can't possibly save everybody. We aren't omnipotent, and we don't have the answer to everything."

"Well, we have to do something," Sarinka argued. "I'm a healer. It's my job to save people."

"Then *you* tell me what we're going to do. *You* figure out a way to reach everybody. And when you do, tell us, because I sincerely would like to know." Hecate's eyes were flashing now. I could tell when she was angry, and while I realized Sarinka was frustrated, she had better watch it because she was overreaching her boundaries.

I stood, smacking my hand on the table for attention. "In the eight years that I have been Queen of UnderBarrow, I have learned a lot from His Majesty and Damh Varias. I want you all to listen to me, and listen well. Yes, we have a responsibility to others—to those who live within UnderBarrow, and to those who live within Willow Wood. Other than my pledge to Hecate, these people are my prime responsibility. But we have to accept our limitations, or we can do nothing. Try to save everyone, and we save no one. We take care of those who belong to us. And only then can we reach out to help others."

Tam stood, holding out his hand. I placed my hand in his, and we stood there, facing the room.

"Her Majesty is correct. We are the heart of UnderBarrow. What we decide, decides the fate of our people. We will make no decision today, except that I will recall our soldiers from Verdanya. The curfew stands. I will send a message to the king of Verdanya, telling him to prepare his people and do what he can for them."

He turned to Elan. "You have a choice to make, Elan. Do you wish to remain with UnderBarrow? Or do you wish to go home? I will release you from your service if you choose to return to Verdanya and your father, the king. If you choose to stay here, you are more than welcome. But make your decision now. We're going to lock down UnderBarrow and Willow Wood. We can't be certain of who might be working with Fenrir."

I caught my breath. "His Lordship is right. When we journeyed to Seattle, we traveled through the Green Lake district. There's a man there who I'm sure will throw his lot, and the Green Lake district's lot, in with Fenrir. In fact, we were going to discuss blowing up the land bridge that connects that district with the Wild Wood. I'm not so certain we have time to do that at this point."

Elan stood and bowed to the two of us. "I cannot speak for Jason, my mate, but for myself I choose UnderBarrow. I gave you my oath eight years ago when I left my father's land for good. My oath stands today." She turned to Jason. "What say you?"

"I am always and forever loyal to UnderBarrow, and to Lord Tam and Queen Kaeleen." Jason smiled faintly at us. "Whatever they decide for the Barrow and the village, I will support."

One by one, each person in the room stood and pledged their loyalty to us. I looked down at Hope, who was curled up asleep in the chair beside Elan.

"Elan and Jason, you don't have to accept my suggestion, but what do you think about enlarging your family by one? She is so taken with the two of you."

Elan and Jason glanced at each other and then smiled. "We've already discussed it, and yes, we will happily take in Hope as our daughter. Aila can help her, I'm sure of it. But I'd like to have the healers look her over, if you don't mind. Who knows what scars are hidden there, behind those innocent eyes?"

With that, we adjourned for the moment, agreeing to meet again in the morning. Until then, there was work to do, and plans to be made, and Tam and I had a lot to discuss about the future of UnderBarrow.

AFTER TELLING DAMH Varias that we would meet with him privately after dinner, Tam and I retired to our chambers. Patrice was there, waiting to fill the bathtub for me and take my clothes. In her presence, Tam and I said nothing about what we had discussed during the meeting. I stripped out of my clothing, gratefully sinking into the hot tub of vanilla-scented bubbles.

"Are you hungry, milady?" Patrice asked.

I shook my head. "I ate during our meeting. Just lay out a comfortable dress for me, and I'll ring for you when I need you. Lord Tam and I need some privacy to talk."

She did as asked, silently leaving the room and shutting the door behind her when she was done. I waited for a moment, leisurely scrubbing my arms and legs, then looked over at Tam who was sitting on a chair nearby, watching me.

"Just when we thought we were coming out of the darkness," I said. "And now, the darkness waiting is far greater than anything we've experienced."

"One thing I've learned, that you surely have also, is that periods of unrest last for a long time. I was alive during the first World Shift. The reverberations lasted for hundreds of years. Nothing settled down during that time. I wonder..." He drifted off, staring into space.

"What? What are you thinking?"

"I'm wondering if Gaia didn't know this was going to happen. I'm wondering if she foresaw Ragnarök coming and decided to strike the first blow with the second World Shift. I wonder if Lyon and the Order of the Black Mist were playing right into the hands of Fenrir? There's no way we'll ever know, but still... So," Tam continued after a moment. "Who is the little girl?"

I told him about our trip to Seattle, including our stopover with Karl the sheriff. "The city's lost. There's nothing left there except ragtag survivors hiding from the monsters, and a few old stashes of goodies that will soon be so much detritus. The old world is truly gone. I felt it more than any other time we were there. The past is sinking into history, and we're on the verge of a new dawn. Or a new dusk, given the current circumstances."

I stopped for a moment, leaning forward as he knelt by the tub, washing my back for me. He brushed over my skin with the washcloth, scrubbing gently, his other hand massaging my shoulder.

"Are you glad you threw your fortune in with mine?" he whispered. "Do you regret taking the throne?"

I considered his question. The truth was, looking back I could see no other choice. Not that I didn't have one, but it was the only choice that rang true to me.

"No. Simply put, I can't imagine a life other than the one I have now. The past is fading, and I'm learning to adapt."

"So I saw today. Five years ago... Eight years ago... You would have never stood up and said that we should keep to our borders. You would have been agreeing with Sarinka."

I nodded. "I'm not sure if that makes me sad or not. I suppose one thing I've learned is that you can't fight every battle. You can only fight those battles meant for you. If we stayed here, if we try to hold our ground against the lycanthropes and Fenrir, to open our borders to everyone who comes our way, we wouldn't be able to defend anybody. We simply don't have the manpower. And I know full well that asking Verdanya if they want to join with us to create a communal front against the danger won't work. Elan's father is too much of a power monger, too set in his ways."

Tam held the towel for me as I cautiously climbed out of the tub. I held out my arms and he wrapped it around me, holding me tight from the back. He kissed my shoulders, his lips pressing against my neck.

"I have learned in times like these, you hold tight to what matters. You take care of your own. And you always tell those you love how much they mean to you." He spun me around, his lips meeting mine. He was hungry, I could feel it, and I lost myself in his kiss, spiraling into the comfort of desire and need. He walked me over to the bed and I tossed my towel to the side. As Tam began to undress, I let my worries of the future go, focusing only on the present, on his body against mine, the feel of his skin under my fingers, and the love that we shared.

WE MET WITH Damh Varias after dinner. He and I had had our moments over the past eight years, but we'd also developed a friendship as well as a mutual respect for one another. Now, I turned to him as much as Tam did. Damh Varias was more than an advisor. He was a sounding board, and in a sense he was living history. He knew every rule and regulation of UnderBarrow by heart, and he considered it his duty to remind us when we strayed from the path.

"So, here in the privacy of this chamber, what is your opinion?" Tam asked.

Damh Varias shifted in his chair. It struck me that the man had never married, and I didn't even know if he had a lover. He seemed wedded to his job, totally devoted to Tam. And he would extend that devotion to me as long as it did not hurt Tam.

"Your Majesty—" he began, but Tam interrupted him.

"While we are within this chamber alone, we are just three friends seeking an answer."

"As you will, Lord Tam. Do you remember when the Fae began to fade out of the outer world? When we had to transfer UnderBarrow out of Eire? We stayed in between the worlds for a long time, while you decided what to do."

Tam nodded slowly. "I do remember. I wasn't sure whether we were going to go back to the Shining Lands, or whether we would remain bound to Gaia."

I had learned about the Shining Lands during my training with Damh Varias after I had taken the throne. It was where the Fae began, and where they returned after they died. It wasn't an afterlife, but a different realm, much like being out on the Crossroads, or in the realm of Chaos. Tam had assured me that there was no way to reach it off the World Tree, and no creatures who did not belong there entered the Shining Lands. But when a Barrow shifted over there, they lost their independent status and went under the rule of the great Kings and Queens. Tam's parents were two of those, I had found out. They had a Barrow in Eire, but it was only a secondary home, a place where they could connect with the Winter Court here in this world.

If we went there, we would be Prince and Princess of Winter, no longer a king and queen. That didn't bother me, but I wasn't sure how Tam felt about it. He loved his parents, but when I had met them at our wedding, they had scared me spitless. I had thought the Bonny Fae formidable from meeting them in UnderBarrow, but it was nothing compared to what I had experienced when I met Lord Aiek and Lady Ishara.

"You think we should return to the Shining Lands," Tam said.

Damn Varias shrugged. "It makes the most sense. We must protect UnderBarrow, and we must protect the people within it. If Ragnarök is truly on the way, no one here is safe. No one on this planet can escape the effects. The Shining Lands offer us strong protection and guidance."

"How can you be so sure?" I asked him.

"Ragnarök may be a battle fought on a few

fronts, but it will affect the entire world. The Jötnar are a prolific race, and Jötunheimr is filled with their kind. Both the ice and the fire giants are deadly and savage, and they live to conquer. With Fenrir at the forefront, leading the way for Ragnarök, they will not be appeased by simply conquering a few places on the planet. They will spread out, doing as much damage as they can. We can't be sure, of course, if everything within the coming war will be firmly based on their ancient prophecy, but if Thor is worried enough to take this to the rest of the gods, I don't think it wise to dismiss his concern."

Damh Varias crossed his arms, pacing the length of the room. "Perhaps we are engaging in hyperbole. Perhaps we are exaggerating the worry. But you have seen the results of the lycanthrope attacks, and now you know who leads them. Can you deny the savagery of this creature? Can you deny Fenrir is a vicious enemy?"

Damh Varias was used to being eloquent, and he made very good points. It was hard to argue against someone who seemed so sure of himself. And in fact, I had little doubt that he was correct. It just seemed such a massive undertaking, moving the entire population of UnderBarrow to another realm. And then there was something else I had to think about. I was bound to Hecate. I doubted that she would hie herself over to the Shining Lands because of me. Would she even give me permission to go?

I turned to Tam. "What about my pledge to Hecate? What if she won't let me go with you?"

The look on Tam's face told me that I wasn't the only one who had been thinking of this. He looked torn, almost in pain. "We need to talk to her. Because Damh Varias is correct—UnderBarrow cannot stay here if Ragnarök is coming. I have my people to think about. But I swear to you this: if Hecate will not let you come with me, then I will move UnderBarrow and then return to your side. Damh Varias can lead in my stead until we're able to return. I will not leave you alone, my Fury."

I wanted to cry. Everything was so messed up. Everything we had worked for was falling to pieces yet again.

"I'm so sick of all the changes. I'm so worn out from this unstable world." I hung my head, tired of feeling so weepy. "I'm sorry I sound weak, but I'm not used to this. I thought it was bad enough when my mother was killed."

Damh Varias said nothing, simply waited for Tam to speak.

"Please send a messenger to Gudarheim, and ask the lady Hecate for an audience. If she cannot come here, we will go to her. But tell her that Lady Fury and I need to talk to her." Tam turned back to me, pulling me into his arms. "Don't worry. This will work—we will *make* everything work out. You are going to live a long time, Fury, given the fact that you are both a Theosian and the Queen of Un-derBarrow. You're going to see so many changes in your life, and you need to get used to it. I know it's difficult, but this is just the beginning of all the changes you'll see throughout the centuries."

"I will send the message, Lord Tam," Damh

Varias said, but before he could take his leave there was a tap on the door. He answered, and Zed entered the room.

"Excuse me, Your Majesties, but Lady Hecate and Lord Thor are waiting in the Blue room. They request an audience."

"Speak of the devil," Tam said, a faint smile on his face. "Tell them we'll be there within a few minutes."

Zed withdrew, shutting the door behind him. Tam held out his hand, and I placed my hand on top of it. Damh Varias took his place behind us as Tam opened the door. Elan and Wheel escorted us to the Blue room.

HECATE AND THOR were waiting, all right, but they weren't alone. Hans and Freya were with them, and so was Jason. Also, Tyrell and the Dagda.

I blinked. Was the convocation of the gods moving into our conference room?

Tam cleared his throat then murmured a welcome to the others. "You have news?" he asked, coming directly to the point.

Hecate nodded. "We do. We called a convocation of the gods and all agreed. If Fenrir is, indeed, bringing Ragnarök to pass, then we will join the Norse gods to defend this place. Prophecies don't necessarily have to come true. We aren't willing to give over this planet to the Jötnar. The gods are going to war."

Chapter 11

BEFORE SHE COULD continue, the Dagda stood. He was a massive god, covered with tattoos of spirals and Celtic knotwork. He wore a leather jerkin over brown trousers, and a torque of gold encircled his neck. On his wrists were matching bracers, and an ornate sword hung in a scabbard from his waist. The Dagda had long brown hair that tumbled down his back, and his eyes were amber, flecked with specks of gold.

"For good or ill, the gods who have returned are united in protecting our followers. We got the call a couple hours ago from Gaia, mobilizing us. Our priests will fight with us, but all other mortals are free to find safety where they can."

I glanced over at Hans. "That means you and Greta—"

"We will be fighting by the side of our gods." Hans caught my gaze.

I knew what that meant. He and Greta would be on the forefront of the war. It made sense, when I thought about it. This was first and foremost *their* war. No one had ever expected Ragnarök to really happen, but here it was, heading right down the path toward us.

"Speaking of this matter," Hecate said. "Fury, you have my permission to go where you need to. I think I know what Tam has decided to do, and I agree that it is most expedient. You will still be bound to me, but I will *not* put you at the forefront of the battle. You're one of my Theosians, but you are not one of my priestesses."

I stared at her, not sure what to say. I was caught between loyalty to my goddess, and loyalty to my husband and my people. I had never expected to be in this position.

"I'd like to talk in private," I said. "But for now, let us discuss matters surrounding the war."

"Your Majesty?" Zed entered the room. He was looking at Tam.

"What is it, Zed?" Tam motioned for him to come toward the table.

"I have a runner fresh off the road from Verdanya. He has news."

"Escort him in."

We all waited, wondering what the hell to expect now.

When the runner came in, he looked exhausted. He also looked more than a little battered, with scratches all over him, and bruises on his face. His shirt was bloody, but I could see no outright wound. He was swaying as though he were faint, and Zed brought him a chair without being asked. The man sat down, waiting for us to speak.

"What news have you?" Tam asked.

"Your Majesty, I was dispatched by King Kesbet of Verdanya. I only managed to make it here because I came under the cover of the deep woods. He sent me out in the middle of the night, and I just arrived. Verdanya is deep into full-scale war. The soldiers you sent arrived, and were swept up in the battle. The lycanthropes outnumber us, if you can believe it. His Majesty Kesbet has no idea of where they're coming from, but they are like an unending force. And they are strong, much stronger than we remember. King Kesbet bids you to send more reinforcements. I'm to take the answer as soon as you give it."

He looked so exhausted I couldn't imagine how he could possibly hit the road again on such a quick turnaround.

"You look so tired. What is your name?"

"Maren, Your Majesty."

"Well, Maren, eat something first, and rest, or you will never make it back."

"Thank you, Your Majesty, but I don't have time to rest. I'll be all right. But something to eat, that would help. And perhaps you have some wirerat?"

Wirerat was a stimulant, made from two very potent herbs and fortified with distilled caffeine. It was dangerous in large doses, but commonly used by runners who were on time-sensitive missions.

"We do have some, but I don't recommend it in your state. However, the choice is yours." I looked him over carefully. When someone was too tired, taking wirerat was the last thing recommended. It could send them into shock, and that shock could be deadly. I turned to Zed. "Fetch Sarinka, please. Ask her to bring several stimulants, including some wirerat. Perhaps we have something equally as effective but less dangerous."

Zed bowed, then headed out the door.

"I cannot send any more men. In fact I was going to send a message recalling my troops. There has been a new development, and King Kesbet must be made aware of it." Tam looked over at Damh Varias. "Will you write up the news in a sealed missive for this man to take back?"

Damn Varias nodded, withdrawing to the back of the room.

"Tell me," I said, speaking to Maren. "Did you encounter anything or anyone on the roads? Are the lycanthropes gathered at Verdanya, or do you think they're scattered through the forests?"

Maren shook his head. "The lycanthropes are *everywhere.* I'm good at my job so I was able to sneak through the forests, but the roads are dangerous. I have no idea where they all came from, Your Majesty. Neither does King Kesbet. The members of the royal family have been sent into hiding." He paused, glancing over at Elan. He obviously knew that she was part of Kesbet's family, but he said nothing.

I decided to ask for her. "Are they all safe?"

"For the moment, but I don't have knowledge of where they were sent, or whether they will be coming back. Verdanya is under siege, and I am not exaggerating. If you recall your troops, Your

Majesty," he said, turning to Tam, "then all will be lost. It is not my place to ask you to reconsider, but Your Lordship, you will be signing the city's death warrant."

Tam let out a sigh, and he turned to me. I could tell that the decision was weighing heavy on his mind. After a moment, he asked Maren to step outside.

"We'll call you back in a moment. There should be a chair out there you can rest on."

When Maren had exited the room, closing the door behind him, Tam licked his lips and turned to the rest of us.

"I would welcome your opinions on what I should do. If I do not recall our men, chances are they will never return. On the other hand, if I do recall them, Verdanya will surely fall."

"I don't mean any disrespect, Your Majesty," the Dagda said. "But whether you recall them or not, Verdanya will fall. The lycanthrope menace has grown, and with Fenrir at their helm, there's not much a handful of warriors can do. We aren't prepared for this. Oh, I'm not questioning the skill of your warriors, or their bravery. But we have not prepared for an all-scale attack."

Tam nodded. "You're correct. They will make no difference to this particular battle. While I am thinking of it, we should send a messenger to the Frostlings, to see how they are faring."

"I'll get on that," Damh Varias said, returning with the missive for Maren. It was sealed, with the official stamp from UnderBarrow. He placed the rolled scroll in a tube and sealed that too. "I've

instructed him to return our men so they may prepare for the coming war. Your Majesty, I have also
offered sanctuary to the citizens of Verdanya who
can make it here within the next few days. If that is
not acceptable, I will rewrite the message."

"No, that's perfect. We're not heartless, and we
can surely do our best to take in the survivors of
this attack."

Zed returned with Sarinka at that moment. Tam
moved to the side to talk to Damh Varias, while I
motioned Sarinka over to me. She sank down in a
curtsey, then took the chair beside me.

"The man outside the door? His name is Maren.
He's from Verdanya. They're under heavy siege,
and he needs to leave immediately to take a message back to King Kesbet. He's tired, and he needs
some sort of stimulant. He asked for wirerat, but
I'm worried that might make him keel over in his
condition. Do you have anything gentler on the
system that will manage the same effect?"

Sarinka lifted her medicine bag onto the table,
and opened it up, glancing through the bottles inside. Finally, she took out two of them. One was a
pale blue powder, and the other was pale pink. The
pink I recognized as wirerat.

"I can mix wirerat with some xoomite. It will
take a little of the edge off of the wirerat, but will
still increase his stamina and ability to travel.
That's probably the safest choice if he wants to get
there alive. Wirerat is harsh on the system, and
if he's been traveling without stop for a while, it's
only going to take a toll on him."

"Will he be able to keep his focus? He's going to

have to slip in and out through the forests because the roads are crawling with lycanthropes." I
paused, then added, "They've launched a full-scale
attack on Verdanya, and Verdanya is not winning."

Sarinka closed her eyes for a moment, then let
out a long sigh. "Then it's started?"

"I believe so," I said. "But please, do what you
can to quell rumors in the village. If anybody asks,
tell them Tam and I are going to hold a commu-
nity-wide meeting as soon as possible to discuss
what is going on." I stared at the table, at the two
bottles, thinking that before long we might all be
running on wirerat.

"Of course, Your Majesty."

I was about to remind her that I was just "Fury"
in private, then held my tongue. Our people needed a strong king and queen. It was time to wear the
crown without exceptions.

"You'll find him outside the door. Give him what
you think he can handle. And maybe a little extra
on top of it. It's vital he makes it back to Verdanya."

As she left, I joined Tam. "I'm going to talk to
Hecate now. Then we need to decide how to break
the news to Willow Wood."

I walked over to Hecate's side. She was talking
in low tones to Thor and the Dagda. She stopped
as I approached.

"Can we talk for a moment?" I asked. She nodded and I led her into an inner chamber off the
side of the Blue room. The servants used it for
staging meals during long conferences, but right
now it was empty. I shut the door behind me and

turned to her.

"You're torn," she said. "You feel you should go with UnderBarrow, and you feel you should stay with me."

I nodded. "I don't know how to resolve my feelings. My pledge to you is above everything, and yet my heart bids me go with Tam and UnderBarrow."

"We have no clue what the next few months are going to bring. The thought of you running out to fight Abominations for me when we're facing Ragnarök is ridiculous. Go with UnderBarrow, into the mists. I want you to be safe and to lead your people. I know how to reach you, so don't ever worry that you will lose touch with me. I am one of the Elder Gods, after all." She smiled then, reaching out to brush a stray lock of hair from my face. "Fury, did you truly think that life would always stay the same? That the world would go on without interruption?"

"I suppose I did," I said. "It's the only life I've ever known. Well, until now. I thought the tsunami and the second World Shift was the end of things as they were, and that we were rebuilding the future."

"You were. But you didn't realize that Fenrir was determined to destroy that future. My guess is that he saw the second World Shift happen and decided to take advantage of it. He's a crafty one, the Fenris Wolf is. He's deadly and always thirsting for blood. It is his destiny to bring about Ragnarök, so he's just following the path set for him. On some levels, you can't fault him for that. He's playing out the tapestry woven for him by the Norns. It's not his fault that they decided he would herald the end of an age. Unfortunately, they decided to stage that end now."

"Do you really think you can stop him? That the gods can join together and stop the Jötnar from coming in?"

"I believe we have a chance. But think of it this way. If you are here, in the thick of things, I cannot focus on what *I'm* supposed to do. We are keeping all our priests and priestesses because they were born to fight for us, but they are bound to the gods in a way that you are not. It's a very different thing, being a Theosian."

"What if I wanted to stay?" I asked. "Hypothetically?"

"I wouldn't let you. UnderBarrow needs you. Tam needs you."

"It's going to feel so odd being separated from Hans and Greta. I'm worried about them, about their safety."

"They are Norse and they must fight in this war. Greta is a Valkyrie and she is an Immortal. She will be needed to gather the souls of those who die. You must sometimes let go of what you love, Fury. You must let people grow into who they are meant to be. If the Norns are kind, they will come through and be reunited with you."

"So...we go to the Shining Lands, then."

"Yes, and you'll take Jason and Len and Shevron with you. Athena has plans for Kendall. And Tyrell, well, the Dagda will decide what he's to do. But you and Tam belong together, and UnderBarrow is in your care. As I said, I will always be able to reach you. If you need me, send Queet. But not unless it's an emergency. As I said, I have to bring all my focus to bear. Zeus and Hera, Athena and Aphrodite, and of course Aries will be fighting by my side. We have been through bigger battles, Fury. Trust us, please."

I nodded, so many thoughts running through my mind. But my tongue seemed tied, and all I could do was stand there. As she started to walk back toward the door, I suddenly threw myself toward her, wrapping my arms around her shoulders, realizing that I was probably so far out of line that she could punish me for it. But I couldn't let it end on just silence.

"Hecate, you have meant the world to me. Please, don't forget me. I will do as you ask. I will go with Tam and UnderBarrow. But don't forget that I belong to you." Tears streamed down my face.

She leaned down, gently kissing my forehead. "I will never forget. There will be a day when I call to you. And it may be soon, and it may be to join the battle. But for now, focus on your people and on UnderBarrow. You and Tam have a village to save as well as your Barrow, and you don't have much time. Leave the lycanthropes and the giants to us. For now, you lead those who cannot fight."

And with that, she gently loosened my arms and pushed me back. "Stand straight. Wear your crown like the queen you are. Stand tall and fierce, Fury, my chosen Theosian. You have your marching orders. Obey them."

I wiped my tears, dashing them away as I

straightened. Hecate reached out and adjusted the crown on my head, and then, bidding me to smile, she opened the door and we reentered the chamber.

LATE THAT NIGHT, with the Sea-Council gathered around us, along with Thor, the Dagda, and Hecate, we hammered out our plans. We worked late into the night, fueled by a constant stream of tea and food, until early morning.

"Are you sure?" I asked Tam one last time.

He nodded. "This is the only way we can save UnderBarrow and Willow Wood at this point. The lycanthropes are too strong, and if they overwhelm Verdanya, which seems likely, we'll be taking in survivors who need care and attention. We can't do that and protect the village with only two-thirds of our guard. We can only protect our people if we take UnderBarrow away from the area."

I yawned, wanting a nap so bad that all I could think about was my bed. But we had things to do first. "When are the heralds going out to gather the people of Willow Wood?"

Tam handed me another cup of tea. I grimaced but took it. I needed the caffeine and the bitter taste set me on edge enough to keep me awake.

"They've been given instructions to gather them at noon in the central square." He glanced at the clock that I kept in the Barrow to keep me on track. "Why don't you take a nap? It's barely eight, so you could get in a good three hours of sleep before we have to be ready to go talk to everybody."

"What about you? Don't you need to rest?"

He shook his head. "I've gone far longer on far less sleep before. But you're still getting used to this way of life, and you aren't Fae, so you don't have our stamina, even though you are a Theosian. Go to bed, my love. Rest and sleep for a few hours."

Elan escorted me back to our chambers, where Patrice took one look at me and hurried over.

"Your Majesty, are you all right? Zed sent word that you wouldn't be back for bed last night, but I expected to see you early morning."

"I'm sorry you were worried. We had a meeting that extended all night long. I have about three hours to take a nap, so please, help me get these clothes off of me, and while I'm resting, I need you to prepare my clothes for this afternoon. We will be speaking to the entire village of Willow Wood, so I need to look authoritative, and yet it needs to be easy to get into. The easier it is, the longer I can rest. I have to be done and ready by about quarter of noon."

She quickly helped me out of my clothes and tumbled me into bed without even a nightgown. As she wrapped the covers up around my shoulders, I wondered if I'd be able to sleep, so much was on my mind. But before she even returned to the room, I was out like a light, deep into a dreamless, heavy slumber.

BY ELEVEN FORTY-FIVE, Tam and I were dressed and waiting for the stragglers to gather at the central square in Willow Wood. The guards had erected a portable pavilion we used whenever we needed to preside over a festival or a village-wide meeting. We would wait until everyone was assembled, then ascend to our thrones and begin the meeting. I was still achingly tired, but the sleep had taken the edge off, along with a dose of Sarinka's xoomite. It gave me an edgy feeling, but had woken me up enough to make me feel bright-eyed and bushytailed. A little *too* bright-eyed, but nobody would notice once we started speaking. I felt incredibly nervous, though, and I couldn't help but wonder what the reactions to our announcement would be.

I glanced at Tam, who stood by my side. "How did your people react when you moved UnderBarrow in the past?"

"The people of UnderBarrow know that I do what I do out of necessity. If there were any complaints they kept them to themselves. But remember, while UnderBarrow oversees Willow Wood, technically they aren't part of UnderBarrow. If they don't want to go, we can't force them. And of course there will be those who see us as turning tail and abandoning them. Either way, their reactions aren't something that we can carry on our shoulders."

I nodded, wondering how long it would take me to develop his cool and composed nature. He had been born to his position, like I had been born to mine, but there was a vast difference between being born to royalty and being born a mutant. Because really, that's what Theosians were—the Sandspit and its rogue magic had mutated my DNA. I seldom thought about myself like that, but it was true.

He gave me a long look. "You aren't scared, are you?

I shrugged. "Not exactly scared. I suppose I'm wondering what they'll think of us after this. Will they respect us? Will they be angry? Will they resent having to pick up stakes and—"

"Enough," Tam said, stroking my face. "What they think and how they react is of no consequence in the long run. They will either come with us and adapt, or they won't. They have those two choices. And those who can accept change, we will accept into UnderBarrow. When we reach the Shining Lands, we'll begin again. It will be easier. My parents will help us."

"I'm sure they will," I said, even though I wasn't sure of any such thing.

Lord Aiek and Lady Ishara hadn't spent much time talking to me during our wedding. And we hadn't heard much from them since then, except for receiving a rather expensive and ostentatious set of wedding gifts. Among other things, they had given me a floor-length fur cloak that put every other fur coat or cloak to shame. It was gorgeous, and I had no clue what kind of fur it was, but whatever the animal, I kind of wanted to see one alive. It was so heavy and warm, and so over the top that I never wore it. I would probably have to get used wearing it, though, given what we were about to do.

The heralds blew the trumpets again and I took a deep breath, letting it out slowly. It was noon on the dot. Time for us to begin the meeting. Tam held up his hand, and I placed my palm in it. With only our fingers touching, we proceeded from the cloaked-off section behind the thrones out onto the dais, and there we ascended the steps up to the hand-carved oaken chairs that served as our temporary seats of authority. The gods were on their way. At least, Hecate, Thor, and the Dagda were coming. We didn't want them here quite yet, but had chosen to bring them in for effect.

Damh Varias stepped out in front of where we were sitting. He held up his hand as I looked around. It looked like most of the village had made it, though I knew there were probably a few holdouts.

"People of Willow Wood, we ask that you listen, and save your questions for later. There have been some serious developments over the past few weeks, and your king and queen bring you news today. Note: there will be no fighting, and no argument. All skirmishes will be put to an end by the guards, *immediately*. We expect your full cooperation, and in fact, no one will be leaving the area until you go through one of the four checkpoints at each corner of the town square. You *must* register with the checkpoint guard before you will be allowed to leave the square today. Lord Tam will inform you as to why."

A swell of whispers went through the audience. Damh Varias stepped back as Zed and Elan flanked our sides. Tam stood, but I remained seating as we had agreed earlier.

"Well met, people of Willow Wood. As Damh Varias said, we have news and it is not good. I will not sugarcoat it, nor am I going to pussyfoot around it. As some of you know, there have been some serious lycanthrope attacks over the past few weeks. This has not been limited to our village. In fact, right now a third of our guards are fighting on Verdanya's side, trying to stave off a massive lycanthrope attack there."

Murmured gasps could be heard, and muttering, but nobody interrupted Tam just yet.

"The lycanthropes will win the battle. Verdanya will fall. I tell you this not to be pessimistic nor to frighten you, but in a realistic assessment of the situation. You see, we have learned that Fenrir, the Fenris Wolf, has emerged into our world and he is attempting to bring about a Ragnarök. He has gathered the lycanthropes behind him, and they march under his banner. Soon—we don't know how quickly, but we know it is coming—the Jötnar will be arriving. For those who do not know who they are, I give you Lord Thor to explain."

Tam motioned toward the enclosure from which we had come.

Thor popped out, his massive hammer in hand. He had taken the time to braid his hair, and even his beard, and he was wearing a flowing red cloak that only underscored his strength and power. He took to the stage in front of us as Tam returned to his throne.

Thor held up one hand to stave off the new swell of murmurs that ran through the audience.

"People of Willow Wood, listen well to your leader. Lord Tam, King of UnderBarrow, is telling you the truth. This is a grave situation, and it's only the beginning. Fenrir is a shifter, he can appear as a large mesmerizing man, and he usually walks flanked by four wolves who keep pace at his side. He can also appear as a massive giant wolf, bigger than this dais, and do not fool yourselves into believing that he bears any compassion. He will eat you alive, be you woman or child or man. He will set his lycanthrope army on you, ordering them to kill what they will."

Thor looked around. The people of the village had fallen silent, staring at him with open fear on their faces. I was relieved. They needed to be afraid.

"As far as the Jötnar and Ragnarök... Allow me to enlighten you. The prophecies say that Fenrir will help lead the world into Ragnarök—supposedly the final battle, but I believe that it's is merely another massive war in the world. It was considered the final battle many thousands of years ago when the Norse people knew only of their own kind. This coming battle will destroy a massive number of lives and bring the Fimbulwinter upon us."

He paused, looking around as the whispers died away. "The Fimbulwinter will be unlike all other winters. The Jötnar—giants from Niflheim—will march through the world and destroy whatever they can. It's in their nature to conquer. The lands will be filled with giants and ice and snow and blood and death. Jörmungandr, the world serpent, will do his best to fight against Gaia. While nothing can take out the Earth Goddess herself, during that battle you may expect volcanoes to erupt, earthquakes to shake the world, everything that you've seen in the World Shift played out a hundred times over. It will be worse than the first World Shift."

Tam stood, scanning the audience. The villagers were staring with stark faces, many of them crying outright. He took a step down to stand beside Thor.

"You begin to understand what we are facing. This is no simple lycanthrope invasion, but a world war brought on by the quest for power. We thought that we were done with that when we settled this village. We thought we could rebuild. But until Fenrir is dealt with, and Ragnarök settled, no one is safe." He motioned to me and I joined them.

"His Majesty and I have made a decision," I said. "We ask you to think of joining us in UnderBarrow. We will be moving into the Shining Lands. How long we'll be there, we do not know. But we cannot, in good conscience, do so without offering you the chance to escape with us. I know that many of you don't know what the Shining Lands are. Quite simply, just as Lord Tam moved UnderBarrow here from the Sandspit, so he will be moving it into the realm of Fae. And you, our beloved villagers and friends, are welcome to come with us, should you choose. You will be required to pledge your allegiance to Lord Tam and to me with unquestioning obedience. We cannot guarantee safety, but we *can* promise to do our best to protect you and help you settle in a space that is not torn asunder by war."

Tam held out his hand and I placed my hand in his. We stood there, facing our people, letting what we said sink in. A moment later, Hecate and the Dagda joined us. I turned, and curtseyed to both of them.

"Lady Hecate and Lord Dagda have further announcements. Please give them your attention." Tam and I retreated to our thrones again.

Hecate stepped forward, wearing her formal robes. She looked quite different in her indigo gown and dazzling crown than she usually did, and far more intimidating.

"The gods of Gudarheim have discussed this amongst ourselves. We have all agreed that we will stay and fight on the side of Thor and Odin and Freya, against Fenrir and the Jötnar. We will not be venturing into the Shining Lands, but instead will stay and battle so that you may have a place to return to. We urge you to pledge yourself to UnderBarrow and take refuge in the Shining Lands. If you stay here, you will probably be pressed into service to fight. For that, I fear, is our only choice: to do battle. You cannot remain neutral. You will either be for Fenrir and Ragnarök, or you will be for Gaia and this world."

There was a shriek at the back of the crowd, and from where I was sitting I could see that the guards were trying to restrain somebody who was having a panic attack. I let out a sigh, wondering how many people would panic and run into the woods and then find themselves at the mercy of the lycanthropes.

Tam stood once again. "Before you leave the square today, register with one of the guards at the four checkpoints. If you have already made up your mind whether you will stay or go, please tell them. If you are undecided, you have until tomorrow morning to make a decision. The guards will go door to door to ask at that time. It will be your last chance. You have until sunrise to make your decision. UnderBarrow can hold everybody in this village if you choose to go with us. Once we have reached the Shining Lands we will set to building new homes and getting everybody situated. As of this moment, we are planning to shift UnderBarrow within the next few days. Events may change our timeline, however, so don't dither."

He paused as a rider galloped into the town square. I recognized him as one of our guards. Leonard darted forward, and after a quick word, motioned for him to come marching up through the aisle toward the dais.

"Your Majesty, Triton has news you will want to hear." Leonard looked so grave that I knew something had happened.

"Come up here and tell us." Tam motioned for Triton, Leonard, myself, and Thor to move off to the side. Damh Varias kept an eye on the crowd as Hecate and the Dagda continued to speak to them.

Triton was bleeding from several cuts, and he

looked exhausted. But he managed a salute and then knelt in front of us, unable to hold himself up.

Tam and I knelt. Leonard kept an eye on everything that was going on, looking nervous. The crowd was unsettled.

"What happened, man?" Tam asked.

Triton looked up at him, tears racing down his cheeks. "Your Majesty, Verdanya has fallen. The lycanthropes have killed the king. Our men were slaughtered. Whoever trained the lycanthropes has trained them well. Only a few of our men made it out alive. They're on the road, trying to get back here. Survivors from Verdanya will be trickling in, the lucky few who escaped. It was a massacre."

Tam and I looked at each other, silent. It was what we had expected, but now that it was here, it made everything so much more real.

Chapter 12

EVERYTHING SHIFTED INTO high gear. Tam and I cloistered ourselves, along with the Sea-Council, in the Blue room. Leonard brought Triton in after the medics looked him over. He was covered in bandages, and carrying what looked like the remains of a large sandwich.

"I see they found you something to eat? Good," Tam said without waiting for an answer. "I'm going to have Damh Varias debrief you in a few moments, but before then, tell me. How many men do you think escaped? And how many citizens do you think escaped onto the roads? I know you can't possibly give us a complete answer, but in your estimation, what do you think we can expect in terms of people straggling in here?"

Triton shook his head, looking defeated. "That's a difficult question to answer. During the siege, they burned Verdanya to the ground. It was a cloud of fire and smoke, and there is no accurate way for me to be able to tell you how many people survived. When I saw the king beheaded, I knew that it was over. I knew I had to come tell you. I don't know how many of our men survived, nor do I know how many citizens made it out. I know there were some on the road, but I also know there are a lot of lycanthropes out there prowling around. Which means travelers are fair game."

Elan let out a gasp. She kept her place, but I looked over at her, realizing our mistake. Her father was the king of Verdanya, and somehow, it had slipped my mind during all the chaos. We should have told her privately before the council began.

Tam must have realized our gaffe at the same time I did. He motioned to Jason. "Go ahead, go on out."

Jason reached for Elan, but she shook him off. "No," she said, struggling to keep her composure. "I want to know everything. I'll be all right. It's just..." Her words drifted off as she caught my gaze. The look on her face was bleak, but determined.

"Are you sure you want to stay for this?" I asked.

"Yes, Your Majesty. Please, let me stay. There's nothing I can do to change matters and we have so much work to do." Her voice was gravelly, as though she might cry at any moment, but I realized that she needed the work to keep herself busy, to keep herself from thinking about what was happening in her hometown.

"If you think you're capable of sitting through

this, you're welcome to stay. But it's fine if you need to take some time." I stared at her, trying to gauge whether we should order her out. But Elan was trained well, and she took her duties seriously. Her father had disowned her, and she had thrown her lot in with ours, which probably meant it was best to let her stay.

Triton winced. I realized he hadn't recognized Elan's connection to Verdanya.

"I did not realize... Your Majesty?" He said it hesitantly, as if not sure what to call her.

"I was disowned. I do not belong to Verdanya anymore, so please, just call me Elan. You said the rest of my family got out all right?"

He nodded. "As far as I know. I don't know where they went, and I doubt if I can find out. But the king sent them into hiding when the attack began. All I know is that they got away safely. Whether they reached their destination, I have no clue."

Elan nodded. "Thank you. But that gives me some hope. I think I know where they went, but it's too dangerous to check."

Leonard turned to me. "Your Majesty, permission to take a scouting party to check on the royal family?"

I let out a long sigh, not wanting to answer because I knew what my answer would have to be. Luckily, Tam took over for me.

"No, Lieutenant. I cannot spare any of our men on what would be most likely a suicide mission. I hope you understand, Elan."

Elan nodded, her lips pressed together.

"Is there anything else you can remember about

the attacks, or about anything surrounding the attacks?" Damh Varias asked.

Triton leaned back in his chair and closed his eyes, as if trying to remember. Finally, he let out another long sigh.

"Two things stick out in my mind, other than the slaughter and the battle. One—the lycanthropes used fire as a weapon. I thought they were afraid of it, but they carried torches into the village of Verdanya like they might carry banners. And I think I saw something else but I can't be sure." He turned to me. "Your Majesty, I believe that I saw several Abominations at the head of some of the troops."

I stared at him. "Are you sure?" *Abominations didn't work with anybody*. They were fairly nomadic, isolated, and pretty much focused on their own agendas.

But Triton nodded. "Actually, I'm positive. I'm good at reading their natures," he added.

I blinked, then remembered that during the first year Hecate and I had set up the training program, Triton had taken it. He had been fairly adept at reading an Abomination signature, and when he left, I wasn't sure what had happened to him. I had no clue that he had entered our guard.

"I remember, you were in the class. So you're certain there were several of them? Were they inbody?"

"Yeah," he said. "They were in-body, all right. They were using lycanthropes as vehicles."

I let out a little groan. It was bad enough when they picked up a human vehicle. A lycanthrope vehicle could take them much farther. Lycanthropes were stronger and more resilient than humans, in every possible way.

"Lovely. Then they have found a way to recruit the Abominations. I wonder…" I looked over at Hecate. "How could this happen? How could Fenrir figure out how to force an Abomination to work for him?"

"You have to understand, Fenrir is chaotic. So are Abominations. It's not out of the question that he can somehow command them. Perhaps through a bribe, or some other way. I'm just glad we know. I'll warn the rest of the gods. This makes the coming battle even more dangerous."

"Shouldn't I stay, if Abominations are helping lead the force?" The thought made me queasy, but I didn't want to shirk my duty.

"No, this makes it even more vital that you are protected from them. You are one of the best Abomination hunters in the country. I cannot chance losing you to a group of lycanthropes headed by an Abom. Besides, remember what I told you earlier? That stands." Her voice was firm and I knew the subject was closed.

"So what's is our next step?" Jason asked.

Damh Varias answered. "Tomorrow morning, we begin bringing those who choose to join Under-Barrow into the Barrow. We also bring in supplies and farm animals. Tomorrow night, UnderBarrow's doors will close and lock. We cannot afford to wait any longer, even for the survivors from Verdanya. And the morning after, we shift Under-Barrow into the Shining Lands. You have twenty-four hours to gather anything you need from the outer world into the Barrow. I suggest, especially since you own a store, Jason, that you gather all of your wares. And your sister, whom I assume will be going with us, should move over her supplies from the bakery. Pots, pans, anything portable that she can bring."

As the discussion settled down to hammering out the timeline, my thoughts drifted off. I thought of Seattle. I had been born there, had grown up and lost my mother there. I'd found Jason, and then I'd found my true love.

I thought about the city that had been my home and now lay in ruins—a ghost city that would never again rise from the ashes. I thought about Willow Wood and how comfortable and beautiful the village had become over the past eight years. Now, once again, we were uprooting our lives. But most of all I thought about the coming battle. Ragnarök was at hand, and I wasn't sure whether I liked the idea of being swept away from it, or whether—in some deep part of my soul—I wanted to stay and fight.

THE ENTIRE VILLAGE seemed to be in chaos as I walked through the central square, flanked by Elan and Zed. Evening was on the way, but the village was as busy as it usually was in the morning, with people rushing every which way and shouts going up here and there.

Jason was at Dream Wardens, once again packing every single piece of inventory that he owned. It was early afternoon, and in twenty-four hours we would be leaving this place. As I looked around at the stalls and the shops and the homes, I felt tears well. We had worked so hard for this and now, it was all in danger.

I dashed them away, wondering why I was so weepy lately, and turned to Elan. "How are you doing?"

She shrugged, her expression grim. "I'll be all right. I wish my father and I could have come to peace before his death, but if wishes were horses, everyone would ride." She paused, then added, "I made sure that Captain Varga and the other stallions were brought into UnderBarrow this morning. They will, of course, be going with us."

"Thank you. I would have hated to forget him. How many so far have decided to go with us? Do we have an idea?"

"So far we have 450 signed up. That's not bad, given the warning just went out at noon. It's only been a few hours. My fear is that the stragglers will truly believe it's not as dangerous as we're making it out to be. But there's nothing we can do about that. We can't force them to go with us."

"Can't you make it a royal decree, Your Majesty?" Zed asked. "Then everybody would have to go."

"Yes, but consider this. Would you want to take people on a journey with you who didn't want to be there? It's neither safe nor wise. Granted it would be for their own safety, but when you come down to it, the truth is that we can't offer safety as an absolute guarantee. We don't know what's going to happen when we arrive, although Tam has sent word to his parents so they are expecting us. But I have a feeling the Shining Lands won't be easy on humans, even if they are safer."

He ducked his head. "Yes, Your Majesty. I see your point. And if we took people who didn't want to be relocated, chances are they might become troublemakers. We have no need for that."

"Amen." I looked around, rubbing my hands together. It was chilly, and I could almost smell snow on the horizon. Raindrops dripped off of the trees from where it gathered and pooled, the droplets icy and smelling almost like mint. Firs and cedars had a certain scent when the rain hit them, refreshing and crisp and slicing through fog like a knife through butter.

"I still feel awkward not staying here," I told Elan. "I never thought I'd be pulled in two different directions. I'm grateful she's not making the choice difficult, but I almost feel cast aside. Like I'm unnecessary."

"The last thing you need to do is get yourself killed by a group of lycanthropes. Or by a Jötnar. Do you know how huge those giants are?" Elan asked.

I shook my head. "Not really. I assume eight to ten feet tall, kind of like Jerako. Only a lot more dangerous."

"The Jötnar are *nothing* like the Greenlings. They're even bigger, and while the Greenlings can be terribly dangerous and ruthless, the Jötnar are just stupid lugs who will happily go pounding things around for fun. Trust me, you do not be facing one of those."

"I didn't exactly have that in mind, but I suppose we have to assume they'll be spreading out throughout the area."

I sat down on one of the benches as we passed by, watching the hustle. Willow Wood had grown up to be a beautiful village, and we had done our best to make it sparkle and shine, but it was time to leave it behind and begin anew elsewhere.

"I suppose every village has a time just like every city and every person. The Willow Wood that we created has turned out to be an interim community." I still hated thinking what would happen to those who chose to stay, but they had been warned. I had to let it go.

Elan seemed to sense the war within. "You have to bid this place good-bye, Your Majesty. Hecate is bound to no one realm. You will always find her if you seek her out."

"I know," I said, watching people scramble to dismantle their vendor stalls and pack up their goods. "Just—some of these people who stay won't be able to survive without us," I said. "It's not just our protection they cling to us for, but we give them food when they can't afford it."

"Those who are meant to come with us will, Your Majesty," Zed said, flashing me a bright smile. I could tell he was trying to make me ease my guilt, and I nodded, grateful for the reminder.

At that moment, Shevron dashed up. She was carrying a bag of sweets, which she handed to

Elan. "Here, I'm giving away most of my prepared things that won't last more than a day or so. Anything that will last up to a week I will donate to UnderBarrow, given I'm coming with you."

"If you weren't, I think Jason would hogtie you and carry you over his shoulder. But I'm glad you aren't making us do that." I glanced at the bag. "What do you have in there?"

Shevron's eyes twinkled. "Gingerbread cookies, and pumpkin muffins."

I held out my hands. "Fill me up, please. I'll take a muffin and three cookies."

As she handed me the food, I noticed there was a commotion over at one of the check-in points. Somebody was arguing with the guard, and he didn't look stable.

"What's going on over there?" I asked.

Elan motioned to Zed. "I'll go find out. Keep an eye on Her Majesty." Elan headed over toward the fracas. I took the chance to turn back to Shevron.

"You know about her father?" I asked.

Shevron shook her head. "No, I haven't had a chance to talk to anybody since the meeting and I've been busy getting things ready."

"The guard that stumbled into the village this morning? Triton? He was returning from Verdanya. You know their king is Elan's father, right?"

"Yes, of course." Shevron narrowed her eyes. "I also know that he disowned her."

"Well, he was beheaded during the battle. The rest of her family went into hiding but nobody knows if they're safe or not and we can't send anybody out to look for them."

Shevron pressed her hand to her stomach. "Oh, how awful. How is she taking it?"

"Like the guard she is. All official and professional on the outside, but inside, I think it's stabbing her. I just wanted you to know because you and Jason are going to need to help her decompress. She's not about to let down her guard in front of me, even though she's one of my best friends. She takes her job too seriously. We need you and Jason to help her cope. Especially during this volatile time. It's not good to carry around repressed sorrow and anger like she's dealing with right now."

"I'll do my best to help." Shevron glanced around. The village was in a mild uproar, people running every which way, carrying bags and boxes. "So, about half the village is going?"

"It sounds that way. I already see some heading off into the forest, though. Probably running off to hide someplace they think will be safe. But Shevron, there isn't any place left that will be safe. Not here. This is it. Ragnarök's going to touch every corner of this planet, because Fenrir is a god. It's not like it was with Lyon and the Order of the Black Mist. And the Jötnar haven't even arrived yet. But it won't be long now." I linked my arm with hers and turned back toward UnderBarrow. "I'd like to make certain you're in by tonight. Do you need extra help clearing out your bakery?"

Shevron nodded. "Yeah, actually I do. Jason's busy taking care of his store, and I'm not about to ask Elan to help."

I looked over at Zed and motioned for him to

come closer.

"Yes, Your Majesty?"

"Find someone to help Shevron get everything moved over to the Barrow. We want her out of her bakery before nightfall. I am not trusting that there won't be trouble when it gets dark. I just have a nasty feeling about it."

I was uneasy, and felt that things were going to go south the moment darkness hit. Those who chose not to journey with UnderBarrow but who expected us to stay and protect them were probably more than willing to take action. I decided I needed to talk to Tam.

"Come with us. Zed will send someone to help clear out your shop. I don't want you running around out here by yourself. In fact, Zed? Send someone over to help Jason as well. And make certain that Aila is in the Barrow, and not helping her father. This is no time to have children running around on their own."

"You really are worried, aren't you?" Shevron asked.

I gazed into her eyes. "I fear a time bomb is ticking, and it's about to explode."

WHEN WE REACHED UnderBarrow, Zed summoned Wheel and sent him out to Shevron's bakery. He sent Fortune out to help Jason. Then he accompanied me back to my chamber, where I found Tam taking a moment to rest. He was lying on the bed, his eyes closed, but I could tell he wasn't asleep. The Bonny Fae were able to rest by putting themselves into a light trance, which was almost as good as a night's sleep.

Asking Zed to go fetch Elan, I shut the door and locked it behind him.

"You have plans?" Tam asked, startling me as he sat up.

"Geez! Scare a woman to death, why don't you? I didn't realize you could hear me. I thought you were *enswaugh*."

Enswaugh was the Gaelia word for their trance-like sleep.

Tam smiled, the corners of his lips turning up. "It does my heart good to hear you speak my language, my wife. But no, I was resting but not fully into *enswaugh*. What brings you back to our chambers? Did you miss me?" He flicked his tongue at me and I laughed.

"I *always* miss you. But no, I wanted to talk to you about something. While I was out in Willow Wood, walking with Shevron, I had a horrible premonition that after dark there's going to be great trouble in the village. Perhaps a riot of some sort. I tried to shake it off but it just keeps growing, and I thought I should tell you."

"Of course you should tell me these things. I trust your intuition. You're a Theosian." He slid his legs over the edge of the bed, sitting up. I sat on the bed with him, wishing it was all over. "Did you tell the guards to keep an extra watch?"

"No, I wanted to talk to you first. I thought maybe you'd think it was overkill or that I was over-reacting." I brushed a strand of hair away from my face that had fallen down from my crown, tucking it behind my ear. Sometimes I still felt like an outlier in UnderBarrow, though it was usually me making myself feel that way. Most of the people had accepted me by now, and quite a few of them seemed to have developed an affection for me.

"We should find out how things are going. Let's head to the throne room for an update." He rang the bell and Patrice popped in, unlocking the door with her key. She was one of the few who had one to our private chamber.

"You rang, Your Majesty?" she asked, dipping into a quick curtsey.

"Yes, help Lady Fury into her official gown. We're heading to the throne room."

Tam went into his dressing room to change clothes, dismissing his valet to do so himself, whereas the outfits I was expected to wear usually required Patrice's help.

"So tell me, what's the scuttlebutt? Have you heard anyone talking about the move?" One thing I had learned over the past eight years was that Patrice was extremely good at ferreting out the mood of UnderBarrow.

Patrice had chosen one of the more ornate gowns, and she held it out as I stepped into it. Try as I might, I couldn't get the damn thing on without her help, but the wide-skirted purple and gold gown underscored my authority, and I wore it when I needed to pull rank.

As she began to hook up the back—there were

105 hooks and eyes—I adjusted my breasts in the built-in bra. The gown was almost like a suit of armor, and one of the few that didn't allow me access to my whip. It had a sweetheart neckline, with three quarter–length sleeves, and it was heavily embellished in gold metallic threads over a purple and black print. It also set off my hair, and even though it was annoyingly heavy, I had to admit, I felt both regal and lovely in it.

"Everybody in UnderBarrow is behind you and his Lordship. But rumors are filtering through the halls that a number of the townsfolk are not happy. They love the protection of UnderBarrow, but they don't want to fully commit. That's my take on it." She finished the last hook and patted the back of my dress. "There, all done. Now let's get your shoes on."

As she knelt with my shoes, I lifted the skirts so she could see my feet. The dress weighed at least ten pounds, and I felt every ounce of it. She held out a black ankle boot with a kitten heel and I slid my foot into it. As she zipped it up, I held onto the bedpost for balance.

"That's all you heard?"

She nodded and held out the other boot. I shifted my weight and lifted my left foot.

"Unfortunately, I haven't had time to go walking through the village. But I am uneasy, I will tell you that. I have a feeling something is coming, something big."

That matched exactly what I was feeling. "Stay close to the Barrow tonight. In fact, unless it's an emergency, I don't want you leaving the Barrow until we move. You are not the only one sensing something in the offing."

Tam returned at that moment, glancing over at me.

"Patrice feels it too?"

I nodded. "And apparently there are rumors that some of the townsfolk are unhappy about this. But we expected that. I don't know, I feel this is bigger than just a riot. There's something out there, looming. I wonder if Hecate can talk to the Oracle." I turned to Patrice. "Will you ask Zed to send a runner over to Gudarheim, to ask Hecate if she can come to UnderBarrow? Tell her I said it's important."

"Of course, milady. I'll do that as soon as I finished your hair."

I sat down at the vanity and she brushed my hair back, coiling it into a chignon with curls draping down from the sides. She affixed my crown, and then stood back, eyeing my face.

"Would you like me to do your makeup?"

I usually did my own, but right now I felt so nervous I thought I would mess it up.

"Please. Accentuate my eyes."

Patrice quickly went into action, and within ten minutes, she outlined my eyes and gave me a smoky shadow. I looked mysterious and somewhat intimidating, which was exactly how I wanted to look.

"Good. This will do. Please run and talk to Zed now."

As she took off, I turned to Tam.

"I'm not sure what's on the move, but whatever

it is, it's big and it's bad. And it feels like it's waiting until after dark."

"The way you talk about it makes it sound like you're talking about a monster," Tam said.

"Maybe I am. I don't know."

As we opened our chamber door, Elan, Shawna, and two other guards were there to guide us to the throne room. Hand in hand, we headed down the hall, in full regalia.

DAMH VARIAS HAD instructed the heralds to sort out only the most important questions, and we spent an hour before dinner answering people's requests. They mostly had to do with foraging for supplies before we moved the Barrow, a boring but important subject.

By the time we were done, we headed back to the Blue room where Hecate was waiting. Patrice had instructed the servants to bring dinner into the room for us, but I was surprised to find most of the Sea-Council there.

"I thought it might be a good idea for us to take our meals together until the Barrow is ready to move," Damh Varias said. "We need to keep on top of everything that's happening, and this is the easiest way for updates to reach all of us. Also, except for your needs, Your Majesty, I have removed Elan from her duties until UnderBarrow is moved."

I nodded. Damh Varias made good decisions

most of the time.

"I think that's a good idea." I turned to Tam. "What about you?"

Tam concurred. "Unfortunately, these aren't going to be the cozy meals that we're used to. But I doubt if we'll find anything very cozy for the next few weeks."

I looked over at Hecate, who looked impatient. She was drumming the table with her fingers, and suddenly stopped when she caught me looking at her.

"I know you're busy, Hecate, but I wanted to tell you about a premonition I've had. I've felt it all day, and Patrice, my maid, has had the same feeling. I wondered if you might ask the Oracle about it."

Pythia, the Oracle, was a temperamental goddess, but an excellent Soothsayer. I had never met her personally, not that I remembered, but I had talked to her priestesses over the years.

"Pythia is not accepting audiences right now, and Zeus has instructed us to leave her alone. She's in a molting season. But I can summon one of her priestesses. She will have to do."

The term "molting season" caught me off guard, and I shuddered, not wanting to think about what that meant.

Hecate motioned to Zed and gave him instructions. He darted out of the room to send a runner over to Gudarheim.

"How soon until UnderBarrow moves? I missed that this morning at the meeting in the town square."

Hecate pulled one of the bread baskets over to her, snatching a baguette. One of the serving girls offered her butter, her hands shaking, but Hecate waved her off as she bit into the end of the loaf.

"Day after tomorrow. People have until morning to report to UnderBarrow if they want to go with us. We'll get everyone situated during the day, and then, come next morning light, we leave." Tam speared a piece of roast beef, staring at it. "Once we arrive, my parents will arrange help to get everyone settled. But it's not going to be easy, I won't deny that." He looked up, staring across the table at Hans and Greta. "We're going to miss you. I wish you could come with us."

Hans polished off his mug of beer. "On one hand, I wish we could go with you, too. On the other hand, the chance to fight by my lord Thor? It's an honor. Perhaps the gracious lady Hecate would not mind sending messages to you from us?" He turned to Hecate, bowing his head. "I assume you're going to keep contact with Fury?"

"Of course, although it won't be on a daily basis. Not during a battle like the one coming. But I would be happy to help out as best as I can."

We were making small talk, trying to calm the tension, as we finished our meal. The servant girl had just served slices of apple pie when the door burst open and Zed rushed in.

"Your Majesty, the village is under attack. An army of lycanthropes has surrounded Willow Wood, and they are led by a great Abomination. I believe the Jötnar have arrived."

I caught my breath. There was no need for an

Oracle anymore. We knew exactly what we were facing.

Chapter 13

TAM AND DAMH Varias were immediately on their feet, shouting orders. Leonard, who had eaten with us, jumped up, panic in his eyes.

"Mom went back to her apartment over the bakery," he said.

"I told her to stay in the Barrow," I said.

"She said she forgot something she had hidden. I have to go marshal the men. Can you bring her back?" He turned to Jason.

Jason nodded, his face set. "I'll get her. You go do what you have to do."

Elan hurried over to his side. "I'll go with you. There's likely to be a lot of bloodshed out there."

I pressed my hand against my stomach, looking over at Hecate, who was on her feet. I hurried to her side.

"They've got an Abom with them. You *know* that I'm the best suited to take care of him."

"No!" Tam must have heard me from across the room, because his shout echoed through the chamber. "Hecate, you have other people who can fight Abominations."

Hecate looked torn but said, "I do, but this one—he's bad. I can sense him. He's big and he's bad and he's dangerous. I'm sorry, Tam, but Fury's the best choice. She has to take him on. But Queet and I will be with her."

"Who's going to protect her from the lycanthropes overrunning the village?" Tam looked furious. He was practically sputtering.

"We'll go with her," Hans said, motioning for Greta to join him. "We stand a better chance of slipping through without being noticed with a smaller party. I promise you, Tam. We'll make sure Fury gets there and back safely."

"Don't make promises—" I started, but Hecate poked me in the side and I realized that if I finished my sentence, Tam might take it into his head to go with me. And that would mean I'd have to keep an eye on him as well. I stopped.

His eyes flashing, Tam rushed over to me. He took me by the shoulders, holding me firmly.

"If you don't come back to me, I'll come after you. I don't care where you end up, I will find you." He looked up at Hecate. "I *expect* you to protect her."

If Hecate was annoyed by his stance, she didn't show it. "I'll do what I can, of that you have my promise. But we better get moving."

Tam turned back to Damh Varias. "Send a contingent out to gather everyone who signed up to go with us. Do what you can to get them into Under-Barrow *now*. Tell them they either come now, or they stay. After you've notified everyone on the list, go door to door, trying to convince the others to join us. Get as many people here as you can. Nobody leaves the Barrow without permission. We're on lockdown. We've just moved our schedule up."

I called for Patrice. "Get me out of this outfit now. Send someone for my shorts, a leather jacket, and sturdy boots. I can't fight in this getup."

Patrice yelled for another serving girl to join us, and the two of them helped strip me out of the outfit as a third girl was sent to our quarters to get my clothes and sword. The hooks and eyes were taking too much time and I finally glanced over my shoulder, grumbling.

"Rip them or cut them if you have to. Just get me out of this thing."

Patrice drew a small dagger from a sheath strapped to her thigh and began ripping the seam in the back. By the time they had me stripped and standing there in my underwear, the girl had returned with my leather shorts, a leather halter top, and a leather jacket. She had also brought my knee-high zip-up leather boots. I crammed myself into the clothes, adjusting as necessary, and then slid on my boots.

As Patrice zipped them up, I checked Xan and made sure she was firm in her scabbard, then slipped her over my back. I shook my hair out, pulling it back into a ponytail. Patrice had scampered off but now she returned with my circlet—I was to always wear a crown of some sort, but this one worked for battle rather than the heavy crown I had been wearing. She affixed it around my head firmly, pulling my hair out from underneath it. I turned to Hans and Greta.

"I'm ready. Let's go."

With Hans leading the way, and Greta and Hecate following, I headed toward the door, stopping only for a quick kiss on Tam's lips.

"I love you. I'll see you in a bit. Don't worry—and that's an order." Before he could say a word, we were off, into the violent night.

THE VILLAGE WAS ablaze. We had skirted the road, creeping through the undergrowth. Luckily, we knew the area and the lycanthropes didn't. But we could hear shouts and screams, and the crackle of burning wood even before we reached the village border. Greta motioned for us to stop.

"I'll fly up and see what I can find out. They won't notice me. One of the perks of being a Valkyrie."

I stared at her. "You can actually *fly* with those?" I motioned to the giant black wings affixed to her back. I had thought they were for show.

"Just watch me." She laughed, keeping her voice low, and then rose into the air, her giant wings sweeping slowly back and forth. I wasn't sure if they were keeping her aloft, or if it was some magic that had to do with them, but she was flying, all right.

As she rose into the night sky, she began to shimmer out of sight and before I realized it, she had vanished. I turned to Hans.

"She really *is* a Valkyrie, isn't she?" It wasn't so much that I hadn't believed it, it was that I had never really seen her in action before. Other than fighting. And I knew she was bad-assed at that. Greta was an Amazon, with a heart of gold and resolve of steel.

Hans nodded, smiling. "It's taken some getting used to, I'll tell you that. But I always knew she was headed for this. She's been training since I first met her. I never expected to fall in love with one of Freya's chosen. Not everyone training to be a Valkyrie is allowed to pair up with a mate. But Thor had a talk with Freya, and she came around."

"I'm glad for both of you." I glanced up at Hecate. "And you too. You could have said no. You could have stopped me from marrying Tam. Yet you didn't."

Hecate nodded, her expression grim. "And his behavior tonight was one reason why I thought of saying no. But it's natural for a man to want to protect his mate. I don't hold it against him. If you had paired up with Jason, however, I would have put a stop to it."

I wanted to ask her why, but Hans shushed us both and I realized we were talking too loudly. I bit my tongue, creeping farther into the bushes, with Hecate behind me. She placed one hand on my shoulder in a comforting way, and I slowly let out the breath I'd been holding.

Hans crouched in front of us, keeping an eye out. The screams from the village grew louder, and I wanted to find out what was happening, but I knew already. The lycanthropes were rampaging, and I could only hope and pray that the guards were getting people to UnderBarrow, especially the children.

A few moments later, there was a noise in the bushes and Hans shifted, silently drawing his sword. But before it was fully drawn, Greta appeared, shimmering back into view. She folded her wings back, shaking the rain off of them, and then motioned for us to join her. Hecate and I scooted out from beneath the bush we had been hiding under and together with Hans, joined the Valkyrie.

"What did you find?" I asked, keeping my voice low.

"I found the Abom. He's with two very large lycanthropes, and I hate to break it to you, but there's a Jötunn with him, too—an ice giant from Niflheim. I didn't see Fenrir anywhere, so I have a feeling they just sent a contingent here to mess with us. Fenrir might have gotten word about us from his cronies who invaded Verdanya."

"Or the other lycanthropes. Any group of them in the area has to know we're here." I suddenly paused, thinking about the Fir Mountain Pack, the group of werewolves not too far from the Frostlings. And then, of course, I thought about the Frostlings. "The Fir Mountain group—I wonder if they've been attacked as well? They hate lycanthropes, and the feeling is mutual. And then, what of the Frostlings? I wonder if Wyfair is under attack as well?"

"You're spinning, Fury." Hecate shook her head at me. "We can only focus on what task is at hand. *Everyone* is going to be under attack before long. There's nothing we can do about either the Frost-lings or the werewolves at this point. We need to take care of our people here, and then get you back to UnderBarrow."

I caught my breath, nodding. She was right. I couldn't help everyone. I couldn't *save* everyone. How often had I given that advice to others?

Queet, are you here? I closed my eyes, reaching out for the familiar feeling of my spirit guide.

I'm here, Fury. I'm by your side. And I will go with you to the Shining Lands as well. Hecate has given me permission. Tell me what you need me to do. His voice was comforting.

I looked back at Greta. "How far away is the Abom? Where is he right now?"

"He's near the northwestern gate. So we have to turn around and go northwest from the village. I have a feeling they entered through the north-eastern gate, and then the Abom and his comrades headed toward the other side to prevent people from escaping that way. No doubt there are also contingents guarding the southwest and southeast gates as well."

At least they were away from the main populace, I thought. A powerful Abom set loose in a popula-tion of panicked people? The thought was stagger-ing. He could eat souls right and left.

"Let's go then." With that, Hans changed direc-tion and we headed off through the undergrowth, toward the northwestern gate. I steeled myself. Time to finish my mission and return to Under-Barrow. Seeing the town square soaked in blood wouldn't do me any good, and it wouldn't help anyone who had died, either. Hecate was right. We couldn't save everybody, no matter how much we wanted to.

THE NORTHWESTERN GATE was toward the agricultural fields. As the rain sleeted down against us, we pushed through the undergrowth, trying to steer clear of places where we could hear fighting. But it seemed like the majority of the conflict was behind us, back in the village proper. We finally reached the fork in the road that led to the gate, so I figured we must be only a few hundred yards from the Abom and Jötunn.

I stopped, turning around to Greta and Hans. "What are the Jötnar like? What do we need to know?"

"We'll take care of the giant, you just take care of the Abom." Hans rested his hand on his sword.

I shook my head. "No. I mean, yes but in case something happens, I need to know what there is to know about the Jötnar. I don't want to be caught with my guard down. Do they have any special powers?"

"This one appears to be from Niflheim, the land of frost. That means he will be able to conjure up snow and ice, and he's immune to almost any attacks using cold weather spells."

I scratched my chin. "Does that mean he's sensitive to fire attacks?"

"Yes," Greta said. "Your fire will work against him. But concentrate on the Abomination. Hans and I can take care of the Jötunn and the lycanthropes."

"Let's hope so," I said. But before we marched onward, I closed my eyes and reached down deep inside for the well of fire that I could feel spinning. I coaxed it out, summoned it to the surface, but kept it chained. It burned brightly, and I whispered to it, allowing it to envelope me, to fill my veins with heat and fury. When it felt like the fire was close to hand—at my fingertips—I let out a long breath and nodded for them to lead the way.

Hecate watched me, nodding silently.

"I'm ready." I slapped my thigh, bringing my whip up. While that might not do much good against the Jötunn, it would work against the Abomination once I got him to the Crossroads.

Are you ready, Queet?

I'm ready. Tell me when and what you need me to do.

We were about twenty yards away from the gate when my Trace screen flared to life. The Abomination was ahead, all right, a murky dark red light flashing an alarm. I paused, realizing that he could probably sense me as well.

"I picked him up. We better get a move on now. Because if we don't go to him, he's going to come to us. The minute we get within sight, distract his comrades. Queet and I will move in and take him to the Crossroads. Hecate, I may need you over there."

The next moment, the red blip began moving toward me.

"He's picked me up. Come on, let's engage. Somebody get out there and draw an cross in the road, pronto." As we thrashed our way out of the undergrowth, Hans drew his sword and drew a deep furrow in the road next to us. He drew another, creating a large cross sign, giving me a path to take the Abom to the Crossroads.

I hurried over to stand by it, forcing myself to avoid rushing to meet the Abom. I needed him here, in the crossroad, and given the fact that we were also staring down at least four lycanthropes and a massive giant, I really didn't have the leeway to make any mistakes. I had to get him on the first go.

Queet, go tease him over here. He'll chase you. Or at least he will if he's like every other Abom.

I'm on it, Fury.

Queet spun out into the road, heading straight for the Abom. The energy on my Trace screen flared. The Abom had caught his scent and was hungry. From where we were standing, I could see the creature lurch forward, but then the Jötunn reached out and smashed him back, stepping in front of him. The giant had to be at least fourteen feet tall, and he was massive with pale blue skin.

"Fucking hell," I said. "They've got the Abom under some sort of control. Did you see that? You're going to have to take out the giant for me to get hold of the Abom."

"We're on it," Hans said, drawing his sword and heading straight for the giant. The lycanthropes tried to intervene, but Hecate raised her arms in the air and let out a shout. The next thing I knew, a brilliant shaft of light shot down from between the clouds, directly onto the lycanthropes' faces. It was moonlight magnified tenfold, so dazzling that it made me wince.

The lycanthropes yelped, one of them dropping his weapons. As he backed away, the giant reached forward and grabbed him around the throat, throttling him and tossing him to the side as if he were no more than a ragdoll. He shouted something that sounded like an order, though I didn't recognize the language, and the other lycanthropes whimpered but forced themselves forward, shivering.

Next to me, Hecate laughed. "So they fear the moon. Then let them fear the *moon goddess*." She stepped to the side, moving in front of me. She raised her hands to the sky, letting out a loud cry, ululating a trail of sounds that spun through the night air. The air currents rippled with her call. Hecate was growing taller, rising into the sky, her indigo gown sparkling as though it had a thousand diamonds attached to it. Her hair rose, writhing on its own, and three snakes appeared around her waist, massive and huge, slithering into existence with her call.

The lycanthropes yelped again and fell facedown to the ground as they whimpered in front of her.

The Jötunn was not as intimidated. Instead, he

simply stomped forward, his massive feet crushing the lycanthropes as he made his way toward us.

Hans and Greta dove in, one on each side, bringing their swords to bear as they fought against the giant. He swiped at Greta as she flew toward him, sword out. She dodged his hand, and Hans took the opportunity to slice behind the giant's knee. The Jötunn stumbled, turning to face the priest of Thor.

"In the name of Thor, begone with you!" Hans went in for another swing but the Jötunn leaned down and swung with his hand, smashing his fist into Hans's side. He knocked Hans off his feet and sent him flying back toward the undergrowth, where Hans crashed against a tree.

Greta let out a war cry, swooping down to stab at the giant's ear. She managed to land on his shoulder, even though she was half his height, but he shook her off, knocking her to the ground behind him.

Queet, while they're engaged, get the Abom over here. Do what you have to tempt him.

On it!

Hecate started moving forward toward the giant, still in her massive state. She could match him foot for foot at this point. I glanced over at Hans, who was trying to pick himself up. But the Jötunn hadn't lost track of him. In fact, he was preparing to land another blow.

"Watch out!" I shouted, hoping that Hans could hear me in the fracas. But I was too late.

The Jötnar smashed his fist against Hans, driving him back against the tree again. Hans slumped to the side, and Greta screamed, sweeping down out of the sky to land on the giant's back.

I was so involved in watching that I hadn't noticed Queet coming my way, with the Abom right behind him.

Fury! He's here! And he's big, be careful.

I jerked my attention toward the incoming Abomination. He *was* a big one, his human vehicle must've been a good six-foot-six, and he was bald, and burly, and looked entirely too strong for me to deal with. But all I had to do was get around to his soul-hole. I had to take him to the Crossroads, though, I knew that much.

Lure him into the crossroad. And the minute I head over, tell Hecate where I've gone. And then join me.

Queet didn't answer, but he dashed toward the crossroad, a flurry of mist and steam in the pouring rain. I held my breath, waiting, arms raised, whip in hand. The moment the Abom landed one foot in the crossroad, I brought my hands together over my head, clapping loudly as I focused on the Crossroads and transported us over.

ONCE AGAIN, I landed next to Hecate's cauldron. The moment my feet hit the ground, I jumped back to make room for the Abom. I didn't want to be within arm's reach when he came through. As he shimmered into sight, I brought my whip back and then lashed forward, striking him across the face before he could move. I needed to disable him before he came swinging for me.

Fury, I'm here. Queet suddenly showed up by my side. Here, he was a whirling, spinning pillar of energy. He sparkled, with ripples of blue and yellow and pink and a faint orange. The Abom suddenly shifted his gaze from me to Queet.

Blood was trickling down the Abom's face, and it looked like I had lashed out one of his eyes, but it wouldn't matter to him. He could feel the pain through the body that he was inhabiting, but nothing would stop him until I managed to either destroy the body—at which point he would be free to jump into somebody else—or to tackle his soul-hole and send him back to Pandoriam.

Check on his soul-hole.

Queet whisked himself around the back of the Abom. *Uh-oh.*

What's wrong?

His soul-hole is closing. I'm not sure why. Maybe the giant did something to it. You've got to get back here now.

Oh hell.

I had hoped to have a little more time, had hoped to have Hecate with me. I wasn't sure how strong the Abomination was, or if Fenrir had done anything to him in order to give him more resilience.

You don't have a choice, Queet blasted at me.

I started to dash around behind the Abom but he suddenly thrust out his fist and clipped me as I passed by him. I wasn't sure how he had managed to move across the eight feet that I had left between us, but one moment he was standing there, and the next moment he was smashing me in the side.

I doubled over, tripping to one side with the weight of his fist.

Fucking hell! Queet, what happened?

I'm not sure, Fury. I don't know what he did. He was there and then he wasn't. Watch out—he's disappeared again.

I blinked. The Abomination had vanished. But as I turned, he was there behind me, and he swung again, knocking me backward, toward the cauldron. I landed, skidding along the road, wincing as the dirt and rocks took their toll on my legs as I slid along the dirt path.

Fury, are you all right?

Yeah, but I won't be for long if he keeps doing this. Can you see him?

I looked around, trying to find some sign of where he was. But the Abomination had vanished again. Cripes, I had never dealt with an Abom who could do this.

I'm looking, I'm looking! I don't... Wait! There, about two yards from you coming in from behind. Dodge left.

I didn't question it, I just did as Queet ordered. I dodged to the left, and this time he barely missed me. Those fists of his were like steel.

I've got to get him to hold still long enough for me to get behind him and find the soul-hole.

I'll see what I can do.

Queet suddenly darted between the Abomination and me. Instead of dancing around, he stayed very still. I suddenly realized what he was doing. He was sacrificing himself in order to help me.

Queet, get the fuck out of there!

No, Fury. You have to take him down now. Hurry up.

Quit being a martyr— I started to say, and then I stopped. Queet was doing exactly what he was supposed to. He was helping me take down an Abomination.

Even as I paused, the Abom started siphoning off his energy. I could see the tube running from the soul-hole in the back of his neck, around to the front, plugging into Queet's energy.

Hurry up, I don't have much time!

Startled out of my paralysis, I dashed around behind the Abom. I couldn't let Queet's gesture go to waste. I brought back the whip, taking careful aim, and lashed out, slicing through the feeding tube and into the soul-hole. I focused all my energy through the whip, all of my inner fire, letting it out in one giant flash as it ricocheted into the Abom's soul-hole. The Abom screeched as a sickly green light began to emanate from the soul-hole where I had hit square center. He turned, howling, and lurched at me.

I tried to dart away, pulling my whip back, but he grabbed hold of the end and he yanked it to him, dragging me along with it. The green flames flickered brightly now, pouring out of his soul-hole, draining him even as he grabbed hold of my wrist and squeezed. I screamed and dropped my whip as the bones in my hand shattered.

He let out another shriek as he leaned forward, drool running down his face from his mouth. The lights in his eyes were dead, and suddenly, there was another rush of energy as he spiraled up, fully out of his soul-hole, and then with one long shriek, vanished. The corpse he had been wearing fell, dragging me down with it, still holding onto my broken hand. I tripped and landed hard on top of the dead man, further dislocating my bones.

Queet, are you there?

As the haze of pain and exhaustion hit me, I looked up, trying to find Queet.

Oh, please let him still be alive. Please, let Hecate get here soon.

But I couldn't see or hear anything, except the drumming in my ears. I realized it was my own heartbeat, thudding so fast that I could barely breathe. The pain in my wrist hit me, and I managed to extricate myself from the corpse, scooting away from it. I looked at my hand, groaning as another wave of pain hit me. It was coming from all directions now, my hand, the bruises on my legs where I had gone skidding across the ground, and the migraine that always seemed to hit after I had been on the Crossroads.

My right hand was swollen, and the fingers looked misshapen, out of joint. I tried to get to my feet but I could barely roll over on my knees, and I couldn't support myself with both hands so I had to crawl along with just my left hand for balance.

As I looked around the Crossroads, barely able to keep my eyes open, I thought I heard a faint music. It was coming from the road that passed Hecate's cauldron, and I tried to call out, but the words wouldn't leave my throat. I could barely think now, barely even remember my name. Then exhaustion from the fight overtook me. I reached out with one last cry, not sure if it even left my lips or not.

The next moment, the sky went black, and I fainted.

Chapter 14

FIRST CAME A light that was too bright, and when I tried to shield my eyes from it, searing pain raced through my arm. I moaned, trying to turn over to get away from the light, but someone was holding me by the shoulders.

Fury? Fury, it's me. You need to lay still.

I struggled for a moment to understand before I realized it was Queet. He was still alive. Well, as alive as a ghost could be.

Where am I?

You're in UnderBarrow. Sarinka is here and she's tending to you. Hecate found you and brought you back. She found me too and helped heal me. The Abom nearly ate me.

Is Tam here?

No, but he knows you're safe. You have to stop moving around. The Abom did a number on you. Not only is your wrist shattered, but he managed to damage your liver. Sarinka can heal you, but you're not going to be out of bed for any length of time.

My liver? I hadn't realized I had been injured so badly. I forced myself to lay back, to quit struggling. I closed my eyes again, trying to shut out the light.

"Fury? Can you hear me?" This time it was a woman's voice, and I could hear her audibly, rather than in whisper-speak.

I struggled to open my eyes again. Sarinka was there, looking down at me. She had healed me up a number of times over the years, but this was probably the worst I had been hurt since the first time Jason brought me to her, so many years ago.

"I can hear you." My throat was raw and scratchy, and it hurt to even form the words.

"I'm going to have to perform surgery on you. Your liver's has been damaged, and I'm going to have to remove part of it, but don't worry, it will regrow, and you'll be just fine." She tried to sound soothing, but the thought of a knife opening me up did nothing to calm me down.

"No! Where's Tam? Greta? Hans? I need to get up. They need me." I started to struggle, suddenly feeling like if I didn't get up right now, someone would die. They needed me to...then I flashed back again. *The fight with the Abom.*

"Fury, you need to relax. I'm going to give you a sedative. Lord Tam will be here shortly to check on you."

"I want to see him—to tell him I love him." I started to cry, suddenly feeling alone with the sudden fear that everybody I loved was fading away. That I was losing everybody.

"I'll tell him. He'll be here and if you're still awake, you can talk to him. But we have to get in there and fix your liver." She held up a needle, and the next moment, a warm rush filled my body as she injected me with something. I tried to fight it, but it caught me up like a gentle wave, and then, I was drifting in a golden fog. I finally gave in to the exhaustion, closed my eyes, and once again, drifted off to sleep.

MY NOSE WAS the first to wake me up. Or rather, the scents of bacon and eggs and bread. I sniffed, wondering why my nose felt so raw inside, and then opened my eyes, trying to blink away the crusts that had formed on the inside corner. I reached up to wipe them, but something pulled when I did, hurting just enough to make me lower my arm again.

"Tam? Tam?" I managed to get the words out, even though my throat felt parched.

"Love, you're awake!" Tam's voice cut through the fog as he leaned over me, his silver eyes wet with tears. He leaned down and placed a kiss on my forehead. "How are you feeling, my love?"

I coughed. "Like I've been run over by a truck. What happened?" I vaguely remembered Sarinka talking about needing to fix something, and Queet reassuring me that he was still around, but other than that, everything seemed terribly fuzzy.

"You had to have an operation. Sarinka had to sew up your liver. The Abomination hit you square on, and ruptured part of it. You also have a shattered wrist and fingers. She operated on your hand, too. But you'll be fine. You'll need some physical therapy on the hand, and you need to rest, but you'll be up and around soon enough." His smile ricocheted through me like the most glorious morning ever.

I shivered, thinking of all the needles and knives Sarinka must have used on me. "What happened? Willow Wood? How is the village?"

Tam's gaze darkened. He hung his head. "Battered. It took a real blow. We managed to beat them off, but they'll be back. Anybody still living there, well...they took their lives into their own hands." He paused, then said, "I don't know whether I should tell you now, but I might as well. We've left. UnderBarrow is in the Shining Lands now."

As the realization of what he was saying hit me, I let out a cry. "*What?* What about Hecate? And Greta and Hans? How long have we been here?"

"We've been here a week. And Greta and... They're back in Willow Wood and Gudarheim. Hecate said to tell you she'll come to visit you soon. I sent word that you survived the surgery." Tam paused, still looking hesitant.

"What's wrong?"

"I don't know. There's something I have to tell you, love." He lowered his gaze.

"What is it?"

"Hans...he didn't make it. The Jötunn punctured several ribs when he hit him. Greta...she had to carry his soul to Valhalla." Tam hung his head. "I'm so sorry, love."

"Hans? Hans is *dead*?" I stared at him, unable to fully comprehend what he was saying.

"Yes, my love. He died helping to protect you. He died a hero's death."

I pressed my lips together, a bitter taste in my mouth. Hans was one of the bravest, most resilient men I ever had known. After a few moments, I asked, "How's Greta?"

"She was... I have a feeling she'll be hunting down giants right and left to avenge Hans's death. Thor sends his regards, by the way, and his thanks for your help. The gods are marshaling armies to fight the incoming invasion. Fenrir is wily and clever. They'll need every resource they can get their hands on."

"How many escaped with us?"

Tam let out a soft sigh. "We came away with four hundred and twelve from Willow Wood, plus everyone who lived in UnderBarrow. I received word that once the dead from the siege were counted, there are three hundred left in Willow Wood. Quite a few died that night. Luckily, we got all of the children who were on our list to bring. And do not worry—Shevron and Jason and Leonard are safe with us. Also Elan and all of our personal guards."

I thought of all the death, all the blood that had been shed, and how the people of Willow Wood were defenseless now. How many would have come with us if we had actually had that extra day? But there was no way to know. And I didn't even want to think about it.

"I'm tired," I murmured, wanting to be alone with my thoughts. I loved Tam more than I had ever loved another person, but I was weary, and I ached, and now my heart ached for all those left behind, and for Hans most of all.

"Sleep, then. Rest and when you wake, you'll be a little stronger. And when you're stronger, I'll show you our new home, my love." He kissed me again, and then Sarinka gave me another shot, and I drifted off into a melancholy sleep.

THREE WEEKS LATER, I was standing by the door of UnderBarrow, with Elan and Zed flanking my sides, and Tam standing in front of me, waiting. I was wearing a beautiful dress, slit up the right side for easy access to my whip. It always returned to me after a fight—we were inseparable. The circlet around my head was the lighter one, easing the strain on my neck. My dress was filmy, leaving me to feel almost naked, but it was warm and sturdy beyond the illusion of being gossamer.

I was healing up remarkably fast, though my heart was still heavy as I thought about Hans and Greta and the world we had left behind. But I had news to offset my sorrow. Something I hadn't told anybody about just yet. But it was time, now that

UnderBarrow was in a safe place.

Patrice draped a cloak over my shoulders as I stood there, waiting to exit the Barrow. I turned to the others.

"Can Lord Tam and I have a moment of privacy, please?"

They blinked but backed off, giving us room.

Tam waited, curiosity flooding his face. "What is it, my love? We'll be late to meet my parents and they don't take kindly to stragglers."

"They'll just have to wait for a moment. There's something I haven't told you." I took a deep breath, gathering my courage.

"What's wrong? Did Sarinka find something else wrong?" He took my hands in his. "What's going on, Fury?"

I squared my shoulders. "Well, she did find something, but nothing wrong. When Sarinka was mending me up, she discovered something else beyond the scars and the fresh wounds." I smiled slowly. "Tam, my love, UnderBarrow will have an heir. Two of them, actually. You're going to be a father. I'm pregnant with twin daughters." My heart raced as I waited for his reaction.

Tam stared at me for a moment, then let out a shout, fist-pumping the air. "Yes! Oh, my love." He gathered me into his arms. "You're serious, aren't you?"

I laughed, extricating myself from his embrace. "Yes, it's real. We're having twin daughters. I couldn't figure out why I was so tired and weepy. Well, this explains why. I suppose I'm going to have to take the next seven months off from chasing Aboms. Maybe it's best we came to the Shining Lands for now." I thought about everything going on back home and shivered. Carrying children in the midst of a world war? I couldn't have managed it, not if I was on the front lines.

Tam turned to the others, beaming. "May I tell the others?"

I laughed, then shrugged. "We might as well." I called back Elan and Jason and the guards.

So there, in front of our friends, we told everyone that UnderBarrow would have two new princesses. There was an uproar, of course, which only drew more attention, and Damh Varias quickly moved in to steer the cheering crowd off to celebrate elsewhere.

I glanced over at Tam and sighed. I missed our home in Willow Wood, but it was time to see our new home. I motioned to the door.

"Show me our new world, love."

Tam nodded, a blissful look on his face. He motioned for Zed to open the door. Taking my hand, the man I loved most in the world led me down the steps of UnderBarrow into the land that would be our new home for however many years it took us to sort out things.

As I stared at the swath of autumn-tinged trees that surrounded us, it hit me. I was a queen, and I was going to be a mother. How that would play into my future, I had no clue, but one way or another, I'd make it work. Because as lovely as the Shining Lands looked to be, they weren't my home. I wanted our daughters to know the land in which I had grown up.

Which meant, there were giants to slay and Aboms to send back to Pandoriam, and a god to defeat. And there, my Lady Hecate was fighting for our freedom, as I waited for the day we could return.

If you enjoyed this book, I invite you to read the first story arc of the Fury Unbound Series: FURY RISING, FURY'S MAGIC, FURY AWAKENED, and FURY CALLING.

You might also like my new Wild Hunt Series—a darker urban fantasy. Caught between the worlds of Light and Dark Fae, Ember Kearney was born with the mark of the Silver Stag. Ember and her best friend Angel are led into a glittering world of conspiracy and danger when they are recruited to join the Wild Hunt, run by Herne, son of the god Cernunnos and the Faerie goddess, Morgana. Now, Ember must not only face her heritage, but she must also preserve the delicate balance between the Fae Courts. For if order isn't maintained, war and chaos will spill out into the mortal realm. Read the first three books: THE SILVER STAG, OAK & THORNS, and IRON BONES. You can preorder A SHADOW OF CROWS.

For lighter—but still steamy—fare, meet the wild

and magical residents of Bedlam in my Bewitching Bedlam Series. Fun-loving witch Maddy Gallowglass, her smoking-hot vampire lover Aegis, and their crazed cjinn Bubba (part djinn, all cat) rock it out in Bedlam, a magical town on a magical island. THE WISH FACTOR, BLOOD MUSIC, BEWITCHING BEDLAM, BLOOD VENGEANCE, TIGER TAILS, MAUDLIN'S MAYHEM, SIREN'S SONG, WITCHES WILD, and CASTING CURSES are currently available.

If you like cozies with an edge, try my Chintz 'n China paranormal mysteries. This series is complete with: GHOST OF A CHANCE, LEGEND OF THE JADE DRAGON, MURDER UNDER A MYSTIC MOON, A HARVEST OF BONES, ONE HEX OF A WEDDING, and a wrap-up novella: HOLIDAY SPIRITS.

The newest Otherworld book—HARVEST SONG—is available now, and the last, BLOOD BONDS, will be available in April 2019.

For all of my work, both published and upcoming releases, see the Bibliography at the end of this book, or check out my website at Galenorn. com and be sure and sign up for my newsletter to receive news about all my new releases.

Playlist

I often write to music, and FURY'S MANTLE was no exception. Here's the playlist I used for this book:

Air: Playground Love; Napalm Love; Moon Fever

The Alan Parsons Project: Voyager; Sirius; Mammagamma

Amethystium: Ad Astra; Shadow to Light; Garden of Sakuntala; Gates of Morpheus; Exultation; Shibumi; Withdrawal

Android Lust: Here and Now

Colin Foulke: Emergence

Dead Can Dance: Indus

Derek & Brandon Fiechter: Imperial Dynasty; Legend of the Dark Lord; Night Fairies; Fairy Magic

Eastern Sun: Beautiful Being

Garbrielle Roth: Raven; Mother Night; Cloud Mountain

The Hang Drum Project: St. Chartier; Shaken Oak; Yankadee; Omnamo; Sukram

Marconi Union: Alone Together; First Light; Flying (In Crimson Skies); Always Numb; Time Lapse; On Reflection; Broken Colours; We Travel; Transient; Weightless; Weightless, Pt 2; Weightless, Pt 3; Weightless, Pt 4; Weightless, Pt 5;

Weightless, Pt 6
   Mythos: Alten Mara; Icarus; Surrender
   Stellamara: Aman Doktor; Resulina
   Tamaryn: Afterlight; While You're Sleeping,
I'm Dreaming

Biography

New York Times, *Publishers Weekly*, and *USA Today* bestselling author Yasmine Galenorn writes urban fantasy and paranormal romance, and is the author of over sixty books, including the Wild Hunt Series, the Fury Unbound Series, the Bewitching Bedlam Series, the Indigo Court Series, and the Otherworld Series, among others. She's also written nonfiction metaphysical books. She is the 2011 Career Achievement Award Winner in Urban Fantasy, given by RT Magazine. Yasmine has been in the Craft since 1980, is a shamanic witch and High Priestess. She describes her life as a blend of teacups and tattoos. She lives in Kirkland, WA, with her husband Samwise and their cats. Yasmine can be reached via her website at Galenorn.com.

Indie Releases Currently Available:

The Wild Hunt Series:
The Silver Stag
Oak & Thorns
Iron Bones
A Shadow of Crows
The Hallowed Hunt

Bewitching Bedlam Series:
Bewitching Bedlam
Maudlin's Mayhem
Siren's Song
Witches Wild
Casting Curses
Blood Music
Blood Vengeance
Tiger Tails
The Wish Factor

Fury Unbound Series:
Fury Rising
Fury's Magic
Fury Awakened
Fury Calling
Fury's Mantle

Indigo Court Series:
Night Myst
Night Veil
Night Seeker
Night Vision
Night's End
Night Shivers

Otherworld Series:
Moon Shimmers
Harvest Song
Earthbound
Knight Magic
Otherworld Tales: Volume One
Tales From Otherworld: Collection One

Men of Otherworld: Collection One
Men of Otherworld: Collection Two
Moon Swept: Otherworld Tales of First Love
For the rest of the Otherworld Series, see Website

Chintz 'n China Series:
Ghost of a Chance
Legend of the Jade Dragon
Murder Under a Mystic Moon
A Harvest of Bones
One Hex of a Wedding
Holiday Spirits

Bath and Body Series (originally under the name India Ink):
Scent to Her Grave
A Blush With Death
Glossed and Found

Misc. Short Stories/Anthologies:
Mist and Shadows: Short Tales From Dark Haunts
Once Upon a Kiss (short story: Princess Charming)
Once Upon a Curse (short story: Bones)

Magickal Nonfiction:
Embracing the Moon
Tarot Journeys

For all other series, as well as upcoming work, see Galenorn.com

Made in the USA
Monee, IL
01 November 2019

16123786R00164